DEAD BEAT

Remy Porter

A Wild Wolf Publication

Published by Wild Wolf Publishing in 2010

ISBN: 978-0-9563733-6-6

www.wildwolfpublishing.com

To my wife Karen for her unending love and support. And to my Mum for believing there was still a writer in there somewhere.

More titles from Wild Wolf Publishing

11:59 by David Williams
A late night radio talk show host is drawn into a dark and seedy underworld

Sinistrari by Giles Richard Ekins
A tale of Victorian horror and murder featuring the infamous Jack the Ripper

Rhone by John A Karr
Gods and mortals clash on Mars

Taralisu by Ryan Tullis
A passionate and heartbreaking tale of a serial killer

Emerald by M L Hamilton
Epic fantasy of gut-wrenching sacrifice

The Killing Moon by Rod Glenn & Jamie Mitchell
The Road meets Mad Max ... Beyond Northern England

Full of Sin by Karl Kadaszffy
Some monsters aren't born - they're made

The Venturi Effect by Andrew Linzee Gordon
After you die it takes seven years for you to go to Heaven

A Sick Work of Art by Claire Lewis
When does art become a crime? How far is too far?

Suicide City by Jake Pattison
A darkly humorous tale of mass suicide in Gateshead

Otherwise Kill Me by John F McDonald
A bloody and surreal story of a schizophrenic doorman

Bully by A J Kirby
A supernatural tale of revenge from beyond the grave

The Stately Pantheon by Kirsty Neary
A dark tale of sex, addiction and power

Turn of the Sentry by A M Boyle
An edgy urban fantasy that will challenge the way you see the world

The Tyranny of the Blood by Jo Reed
A dark fantasy dealing with time travel, hereditary madness and eugenics

The King of America: Epic Edition by Rod Glenn
A futuristic thriller of betrayal and redemption amidst an America gripped by revolution

FOREWORD

Most police officers I know don't advertise the fact. It's not because they're ashamed of their chosen profession; they take pride in a difficult job. It's not out of fear; they regularly place themselves in danger to protect the general public. No, the police officers I know are courageous and admirable people. I think the reason they don't advertise their professions is that they want to be treated the same as the rest of us.

It's amazing how quickly attitudes can change when we find out someone is in law enforcement. It's often a subtle shift. There's a certain reticence to be natural around them. Maybe we're scared we'll blurt out some past misdemeanour. Maybe we need to polarise things into them and us. Whatever the reasons, our attitude towards the person changes. And yet, for all their training and professional standards, they are no different from us. They have the same drives, they live the same lives and they make the same mistakes.

In *Dead Beat*, Remy Porter has given us an all too human hero in PC Johnny Silverman. At first, he may not appear to be an everyman character. As a police officer, he is a paragon of justice, a pillar of society, a manifest representation of integrity. However, behind this façade is a flawed human being just like you and me.

When the zombies start to bite, like the rest of the world, Johnny is thrown out of his depth. As the survivors coalesce round the sleepy community of Haven, fending off the putrid attacks of the undead, Johnny finds himself on uneasy ground. The old rules of law and order are thrown into disarray. Johnny wants to carry on with his vocation of helping people, but ultimately what sanction does he have? When the moral compass of a society is suborned for the need to survive, what mandate does Johnny have?

Dead Beat kept me off kilter the whole way through with a stream of well integrated themes and characters. The early chapters of the book are reminiscent of a crime novel with the protagonist's routine as a cop on the beat in a rural village. But as the plot develops, we find ourselves immersed in a western style morality play with the sheriff pitted alone against the powerful clan who ride roughshod over the town's folk. Then we're thrown into an action movie climax. While all the time from the first page to the last we are given the unadulterated terror of the undead.

Remy Porter gives us a flurry of the tiniest details that bring the reality of the undead to life. His writing is replete with throwaway glimpses of the apocalypse. And for me it's these details that support the believability of the world he has created.

In the same mould as Romero, the zombies here are the slow shambling unremitting monsters we have all come to fear. But the real horror in *Dead Beat* isn't so much the walking dead or the gruesome descriptions, unsettling though they are. The true horror is the sick and warped personalities of some of the characters and the utterly believable perversions, vendettas and murderous natures Remy exposes. The downfall of society may allow some to forget their past and strive boldly into the future, but this is not always a positive act. The small degrees by which the characters justify or rebuff their vile actions and how those transgressions fester and turn people more rotten than the besieging zombies is all too credible. This is not a redemptive story; it does not preach a moral. It left me feeling haunted and saddened.

It is a tribute to Remy's writing style that ultimately what disturbed me most was not the revulsion at the soulless zombies, but the dismay at man's inhumanity.

This zombie novel is on a par with David Moody. It is fast paced, engaging and will repulse and disturb you like a good horror should.

Iain McKinnon, June 2010

PROLOGUE

Trevor had finished his checks on the top of the red diesel tank, and climbed down the narrow, steel ladder to the base. He adjusted his fluorescent yellow security tabard and rooted in his pockets for smokes.

'It's not a bad job we do,' he said to himself, looking up at a starry sky. The near full moon gave the fields surrounding the water treatment plant almost a daylight glow.

'Check completed at tank four, Richard,' he said into his walkie-talkie.

'Roger that. Another quiet one hey Trevor? Come back in and let me beat you at cards.'

'Good idea, Richard. I owe you a shoeing from the last time you fleeced me.'

The radio crackled silent again. Trevor wondered if he had put his foot in it again with the little man. Richard could be so sensitive. He shoved the radio back into his pocket.

He walked over to the fence and the dry stone wall below it. Trevor liked the night view down over the empty fields and the rolling hills on the horizon. There wasn't another house for miles; it was refreshing. The bosses still hadn't replaced the barbed wire in this section, he thought, accompanied with an audible tut. Red diesel had been taken last month, not that anybody really cared. It wasn't his problem to worry about such things. Trevor drew in a long drag of smoke, his sallow cheeks pinching inward.

'Yes, not a bad job we do,' he mumbled again. After twenty years as a postman, this was infinitely preferable; a lazy job working as a night security officer in a sleepy water treatment plant. Nothing happened at night; the machines all ran themselves. The money wasn't stellar, but with his postman's pension he did well enough. There were certainly far worse ways to spend forty hours a week.

Stamping out his cigarette butt under his boot heel, he mashed it down with all the others he'd left. Nobody would complain. Turning to leave, something caught his eye, and Trevor turned back to the fields. Peeping over the dry stone wall was a woman's face, pale in the moon light.

'What are you ...' he began to say, but a flash of light stopped him.

Trevor felt pain in the centre of his chest, and wondered for a second if this was a heart attack. His knees gave way and he fell down onto the grassy earth.

'Finish him now,' a man said, an American twang.

Trevor heard the fence jangle as others climbed over. He found himself staring up at the night sky, and at all the stars he wished he could name. His head felt too heavy to turn. Something bad was happening.

There was the woman's face again, leaning in, offering him something. There was that flash again...

CHAPTER 1

Old people smell like mould, was Tracey's overriding impression of her time at the residential home, Sanctuary Retreat. It could only get worse. Today was all about making tea and washing dirty linen, but bed baths and adult nappies bobbed ominously on the horizon. It was a terrible job, a stopgap, she told herself, until she figured out what the hell to do with her life.

She pulled the brown plastic dish out of the microwave and made room on the tray. If she never had to eat such a sorry mixture of watery potato, peas and dried meat in her lifetime it would be all too soon. The radio news babbled on about a riot at a university in Manchester, students protesting the war in Afghanistan again no doubt. *Bag o' shite.*

Tracey rooted through drawers looking for the plastic knife and forks, still unsure where everything was after four weeks. She found them next to the sink and caught a look at herself in the grimy mirror. The kitchen humidity made her face look pale and greasy. Must knock those takeaways on the head, she said to herself. The cheap yellow nylon uniform stuck to her in the wrong places, short sleeves riding up to show a hint of a sparrow tattoo on her shoulder.

Tracey lifted the tray and pushed through the swing door. Mrs. Barnicott's room was upstairs somewhere in the maze of corridors of the old Victorian house. The décor was nasty, worn crimson carpets and too many pictures of laughing cavaliers. The corridors were narrow and claustrophobic, fanning out in a crazy rabbit warren. Room numbers appeared placed at random and she felt she spent half her time at Sanctuary Retreat taking wrong turns.

She spotted Mercy, the woman from the Dominican Republic who had been working there for forever. She was in a room making a bed while a ninety year old guy stood waiting, one leg trembling to an unheard beat. Mercy had been asked by the boss to show her the ropes but had quickly abandoned Tracey in the kitchen as soon as he'd left for the day.

'Lost again, Mercy? I'm taking this up to Mrs. Barnicott. I think I may have to re-heat this shit.'

Mercy looked over from the bed. 'Nah, screw that, Trace. Agnes Barnicott don't care what the fuck she puts in her mouth. Caught that bitch eating sticky shit off her slipper just the other day. Dump the slop and we'll watch *Loose Women*.'

Mercy pointed her in the right direction and Tracey found the door she wanted. She knocked out of politeness and walked in.

Fuck.

Mrs. Barnicott had gone.

Tracey pushed the tray onto a dresser, dislodging black and white photographs with a clatter. Checking the far side of the bed and then the wardrobe, there was nothing to see but old dresses smelling of rot.

Tracey ran out and back tracked. 'Mercy, we have a problem!'

'Okay you do downstairs and I'll go through bedrooms. Fucker's playing hide, go seek.'

Tracey checked the outside doors. It wasn't unknown for oldies to take a wander into the village. Her boss would be incandescent, that she knew.

The doors were locked.

The lounge had old people in but no Mrs. Barnicott, likewise the dining room. Nowhere left, she thought, and went to phone the police. Standing with the receiver in her hands, she cupped it to her ear. No dial tone. Worried, she noticed the cellar door. In her time at Sanctuary Retreat she'd walked past the heavy white door dozens of times. She had even tried it once out of curiosity and found the handle seized up and immovable. Now it was open an inch.

'Mercy,' she called upstairs, feeling a sudden case of heebie jeebies. No reply.

She opened the door and peered down. The dust rose up and invaded her nose. Tracey let go with a flurry of sneezes. Always she had this reaction to dusty rooms.

'You down there Mrs. Barnicott?'

She took a step onto the creaking wooden steps, her left hand fumbling for the cobwebbed light switch. A low watt bulb fizzed into life below. Tracey was surprised at how far down the steps went.

'Mrs. Barnicott,' she shouted.

One slow, creaking foot after another. Her hands reached out to steady herself, touching more old spider webs on the rickety banister rail. Halfway down she saw the boxes stacked on the shelves against the cellar wall. One of the boxes was for an old Spectrum 48 computer, the 80's computer with rubber keys. She knew it because her older brother had owned one.

She was below the ceiling height of the cellar room now. There was a figure there standing still, facing away. She was in a nightdress and had bare feet. Tracey saw the grey skin and put it down to the poor light. White hair clumped and matted.

'Mrs. Barnicott?'

Tracey saw her turn and bare her teeth. The hanging bulb shattered as the old woman's head cracked through it. Everything went black bar the burned print of the light on her retinas. Tracey turned on her heels and went to run up the stairs, but one foot missed a step and instead she fell onto her knees. She clawed at the stairs determined to climb.

Mrs. Barnicott was biting into her leg; white hot pain shot through her body. She flailed her legs wildly but couldn't shake her off.

She screamed up to the door but it was already closing.

CHAPTER 2

I checked the fuel gauge.

Bastard.

The last one in had left it quarter full. I'd need a trip out of the town now to fill up before the end of my shift. Now where was that fuel card hiding? I thought to myself, reaching around and making the police 4x4 swerve.

Over the crest of the hill, I left the village behind me. The country road arced down giving a fine view of a crumbling Pele tower. Built in the 14th century, it was the oldest building in the parish. There was an estate car parked in the lay-by nearby. A tourist couple in matching red Berghaus looked ready for the walk up.

I passed them by and the road cut through the green fields leading to the coast. Rain spray washed over the windscreen.

The airwave radio set in the vehicle hissed with static. The mast down with an unknown fault, it had been hours since I last heard from the control room. Stretching over the wide seats, I took another bite out of my diet bar. I was bored and unmotivated, the stubble on my face itched for a shave. Turning right off the main drag the Freelander hissed onto the gravel lane that led to the beach. I passed two old cottages on either side but didn't see any people. The rain was starting to lash down and the sky appeared grey and cold, like a tramp's dirty blanket.

'Zulu alpha two six at scene,' I said into the terminal clipped to my fluorescent stab vest.

Silence.

Parking, I pulled my heavy waterproof off my kit bag on the back seat. The horseshoe bay sat in the distance, and I could already hear the fizz of the surf on the rough shale. The path disappeared into the woods and I stepped carefully around exposed roots and smooth limestone. Mud splashed over my heavy boots, another job for later.

The incline became steeper and opened out onto a cliff path. Picking my way down I stepped onto the beach, White Creek.

In the surf line, I could see the body.

Walking closer, I saw the thin pelt was wet and shimmering and its round shape rolled sideways with each wave break. There was a thin foam of bloody bubbles poised in its lips. I jumped back when it gave a rasping snort. Looking back towards the shoreline, I wondered which crazy person had left this note for me at the police station. All I saw was the dark forest stretching back from the cliff wall far up the hill.

The seal coughed again. The clotted sound was louder than before and more blood bubbled out of its mouth. I nudged a large rock with my boot and considered using it but when I looked down again the creature had already died. The council needed to collect the body. I wondered how I would tell them.

Something else was there in the water. A green glaze, like a chemical spill pooling around the carcass.

Fumbling in my coat pocket, I pulled out an assortment of dirty tissues and crumpled fixed penalty tickets. In the detritus was a small white strip of bio-chemical paper left over from some half-forgotten training exercise months ago. I dipped one end into the day-glo water. It turned purple. Probably this was bad, but I couldn't remember what it meant. I made a mental note to look it up later.

Straightening up I sighed. The village beat in Haven was painful. Why I'd ever agreed to transfer here from the local town I didn't know. Neighbourhood policing was a slow death.

Squinting back at the tree line, it felt like somebody was watching. Too far to make a person out, it was all trees and shadows.

I was pacing back towards the cliff when the airwave finally spoke.

'… response to Tomlinson's,' Control crackled.

'Repeat?' I shouted, breaking into a jog.

The 4x4 wasn't great for blue light runs. It was heavy and unstable, like putting a breeze block onto roller skates. Pushing it wild and reckless, this was really the only perk of the job for me these days.

Hammering back up the track, I went onto the main road to the village. In my peripheral vision I could make out the tower again, and a flash of red clothing from the two tourists who were almost there.

The drop into the village was equally fast.

Haven was home to two thousand people. It was, to all intents and purposes, a retirement village with a very aged population. Large Victorian houses in the main, scattered haphazardly over a green hillside. Two pubs, five shops and a newsagent just about summed it up. Add to the mix one crumbling station house.

Tomlinson's was the smaller of the two supermarkets in the village and had been a Spar, a Co-op and many other incarnations over the decades whilst always selling exactly the same corner shop tat.

Two old women milled about outside. 'The shop is closed up and it's 8.50. It should be open at 8.00 and there's mess all on the floor. Look at the floor, Officer. Look at the mess,' one said.

Cupping my hands against the front door window, I looked into the gloom. The place looked ransacked; I could see broken bottles and cans all over the aisles. No sign of Mrs. Tomlinson, the owner who lived in the flat above.

No back up to call, I rammed my shoulder into the door and felt it give easily. The two biddies moved as if to follow me inside.

'Wait please ladies. It could be a burglary, it could be anything.'

Further inside, broken glass and spilled dry pasta crunching under my boots. I looked at the till for the signs of a break in, but the area was untouched.

'HELLO, IT'S THE POLICE,' I yelled.

A shuffling sound came out of the stock room at the back. Moving closer I drew my extendable baton.

CHAPTER 3

Alison Henderson put her hands on the cold steel lever and pulled open the field gate. Underfoot, the path was clogged with mud and animal waste moistened by rain. She buttoned up her red coat another notch and waited for her husband Derek to catch up. He was a slow man at the best of times.

'The tower looks great. 14th century you know,' he said.

'Yes, you said that already, dear.'

She looked away towards the tower; an underwhelming mass of crumbled and weathered grey limestone three storeys in height. She thought it quite an apt symbol for their twenty year marriage.

Most of the walls had fallen and she had heard that the roof had been taken some 150 years earlier for the farmhouse she could see nestled in the small valley half a mile away. She looked around for other houses, but there were none. On the road, she saw the flashing blue lights of a police vehicle in a rush to some emergency or other.

Only one side of the tower still stood upright. On it a sign screwed to the wall read, 'DANGER OF FALLING STONE. DO NOT ENTER.'

Through the holes in the wall, she could see worn stone steps leading up what remained of a turret. At the base, a locked metal gate blocked easy access. To stop the kids, she thought.

They walked nearer the site, the wind gusting rain into their faces.

'Impressive, isn't it!' Derek said.

She wasn't really interested and her eyes wandered away, where the path next to the tower led to a wooden stile and more woods. Far beyond that she could just make out the roofs of caravans from the nearby caravan park.

Derek asked for a picture; he was obsessive like this. Through the viewfinder, the rain obscured the picture forcing her to wipe the lens crudely on her sleeve. Trying again, she sighted her husband with one foot on a fallen piece of wall. Behind him, the tower filled out the frame.

There was something else, and she lowered the camera to see with her own eyes. Squinting into the rain it looked nothing more than a bundle of rags blown over the wall, but then the rags stood up. Alison was amazed to see it was a woman with an odd stiff-legged walk.

'What's wrong with her?' Derek whispered.

Derek approached the strange woman, open and jovial. He was the fifty-five year old husband with the practised people skills for every occasion, her Derek, the meeter and greeter of the family.

'Quite a tumble you had,' were his last words.

The woman in the yellow uniform had eyes like black pebbles in a china doll's face. Dry blood and vomit streaked her laughter lines like a rich broth. On her chest appeared a nametag, TRACEY.

At that moment, another bundle came over the stone wall, followed by another.

'Derek!' she shouted.

He seemed paralyzed and helpless out there.

Tracey pushed Derek over as if he was nothing and straddled him almost sexually. Alison heard Derek's screams as Tracy tore at him with her mouth. The other two figures came nearer, as doll-like as she was. They didn't stop for Derek, they moved for her. Beasts. Their mouths and teeth frothing with juices.

Alison turned and ran for the tower. Her instincts taking her to the only place there might be safety. A few strides and there was the locked gate blocking her way up the tower steps. Frantically she pulled and rattled it, a rusted padlock taunting her.

A few seconds left, stretched out like an eternity as her whole being flooded with adrenalin. Alison's hands gripped the wet limestone and her feet scrabbled on the gate for purchase. She lifted and pulled as the things came reaching for her. A cold hand gripped at her boot. Seven feet from the ground she clung by her fingertips. Her boot pulled away, and she propelled upwards, out of control and over the top.

Falling down onto the cold steps, the back of her head made a dull crack on the smooth stone. She was winded and couldn't breathe. The grey hands reached for her, a cold touch on her cheek. She breathed out deep and fast, the back of her head felt sticky with blood. Dazed, she watched the thin steams of red diluted quickly by the rain.

Alison crawled away from the reaching hands and the inhuman sounds. At the top of the stone steps she looked out at the view through jagged holes in the walls. She could see chimney smoke rise from the farmhouse in the valley.

'HELP ME!' she shouted, but the wind whipped it away.

She sat on the cold steps and wept. No phone or food in her pockets.

Alone now.

The three monsters at the gate were joined by a fourth, its ripped red jacket still dripping fresh blood. Derek's small intestine hung out like a child's skipping rope. One eyehole torn and his nose just barbed and serrated gristle. He smiled up with a mouth of broken teeth.

A hungry smile.

CHAPTER 4

June Tomlinson was a widow who had owned this shop for all of the five years I had been a policeman for the village. She had a kindly way about her and a habit of handing out free sweets to children shopping with their parents. I saw her stumble out before I got to the storeroom door, cheek torn open from eye to mouth. Mrs. Tomlinson moved like a mindless ballerina, crashing off shelves, heading inexorably towards me.

The hag lunged, a black gruel flowing from her guppy mouth. Staggering back on my heels, I backed into the main food aisle, all but falling over the feet of another body. The young shop assistant, forteen years old, was face down in a congealed pool of his own blood. The boy's neck was bitten clean through like an unlucky gazelle in a lion documentary. Twitching and somehow still alive. I didn't stop to look too closely. Sidestepping, I made it all the way back to the open display fridges.

Mrs. Tomlinson was too quick; I raised my baton and brought it down with everything I had as she barreled into me. The baton end sliced across the side of her face, gouging deep into one eye and making it burst out like a wet pustule. It had no effect and she had me off my feet. Her teeth started ripping at the stuffing on my Kevlar stab vest.

I tried pushing her head away, but she was too strong. The witch between my legs like something out of a porno horror movie, my hands searched desperately on shelves for a weapon to make her stop. No luck. All that I could grasp were packet sauces and custard.

Her teeth gnashed like a frenzied dog and her flecks of spittle went into my mouth. *Bitter almonds.* Pinned down, I was becoming helpless.

'HELP ME!'

An old Ju Jitsu move came to me like manna from heaven. I raised my heels towards my ass and dug them in, then shot my hips up and to the side in one explosive motion. I reversed my position on the old hag and now we were together in missionary.

Her fevered biting motions wouldn't stop, but now she was chomping on fresh air. Green tinged, her hands lashed and racked at me in painful but uncoordinated slaps.

Grabbing a tin of beans, I smacked it into her forehead, shocking myself at the dent I'd made in the old woman's head. I suspected professional standards would have something to say about this.

Mrs. Tomlinson didn't seem bothered and stood up for round two. She lunged again but missed, I backed into the young shop assistant who was somehow on his feet. The boy's neck was too torn to support his head's full weight, and it lolled to one side at a jaunty angle.

What the hell was going on? I ran out the shop door and pulled it closed behind me. Both Tomlinson and the rip-neck boy collided with the door, like birds bouncing off a windowpane.

The old women had disappeared. I realized why when I saw more broken people stumbling my way. Six bloodied bodies coming out of their neat Victorian gardens, moving for me.

I pressed the red emergency button on my Airwave radio. It should have given me ten seconds of free mic for everyone to come running. It was either broken or there was nobody listening, I was out of time.

'This is Zulu Alpha two six requesting back up at the Tomlinson's, Haven,' I shouted repeatedly as I ran for the 4x4.

I fumbled for the key fob to get me into the vehicle. There were normal people running, the screech of tires as cars in a hurry tried to get away. The same terrified faces passing …

My key fob just wasn't working; my hands wouldn't obey me. One old man with his dentures half in, half out of his mouth ran at me. He had the speed no eighty year old should possess. My right foot went up in a rough approximation of a side kick. The old man ran through it, momentum slamming my back painfully into the 4x4, and making the glass in the rear driver door shatter. The old man fell away, giving me the chance to press the fob. Already there was a woman in a bloodied bra top jumping onto the bonnet.

Fumbling with the starter buttons, I brought the 4x4 to life. I tore forwards, nearly hitting another car looking for a speedy exit. The woman on the bonnet raised a bloody hand to attack but lost her grip. I felt the 4x4 bump twice over the top of her, but I wasn't for looking back.

I couldn't believe what was happening. I went for my radio again but this time felt the cracked plastic casing; it was dead from the struggle in the shop. I tried the vehicle radio set and when it came on there was nothing but a cacophony of noise, nothing but awful screams and animal sound. Then with an electric 'ping' the airwave went out like a light. *What the hell was happening?*

Wheeling left down the main street, I headed for the police station. Pulling my mobile phone out of my pocket, I held it up to my face.

No service.

CHAPTER 5

The old station house was a detached two storey limestone building with heavy key coded doors and steel bars on the windows. It had two detention cells that weren't officially used anymore. All prisoners went to the larger, modern police station in the town of Havelock ten miles away.

More bodies filled the road and I swerved a crazy slalom course into the rear station house car park. Hitting at least two of them, I knocked them spinning into a heap with the side of the 4x4.

Jumping out of the car and left the driver door swinging open, for a split second registering the Jackson Pollock red splatter down the length of the vehicle. Running up to the station's back door, I punched the key code, red light. Typing again, I watched the bodies begin to funnel towards me. I had seconds.

'COME ON!'

The number and letter jumble entered, the silver box paused, considered and then finally turned the handle light green. Inside I slammed the heavy oak door behind me.

This was the equipment room for the police constables and police community support officers. I was surrounded by large pigeon holes stuffed with black kit bags and fluorescent coats and vests.

There were eight police constables and four Police Community Support Officers at the station, but as it was Sunday next to nobody was at work. Loud banging startled me, hands on the door. Lurching forward, I found the light switch.

'Hello? Who's that? Who's there?'

I followed the voice into the next room and found Summer Harris, the local village PCSO curled up in a ball next to one of the computer desks. She was a small, petite bottle-blonde, twenty one years old. Her eyes and cheeks were red raw with tears.

'Christ, are you okay?' I crouched down, made her flinch.

'Have they bitten you Johnny?'

'No, it's just a scratch,' I said, uncertain, blood and grazing on my knuckles. My vest hung in strips, and looked like it had been through some kind of shredder.

'No bites, Summer, I promise.'

'I've been trying to ring home but the phones won't work,' she said. 'What the hell is going on?'

'No idea, but we're safe here I think. This place is Fort Knox. Don't think it's just the village, screams on the radio came from Havelock too.'

'Just want to get home, Johnny. I don't know what's going on but I don't want to stay.'

'Give me a minute, Summer. Who else is in the building? We need to get everyone together.'

'Rogers went out in the van this morning and hasn't come back yet. Sergeant Dolan went out on foot to a job; I don't know where he is now. The computers, the phones Johnny, nothing is working. What the hell does it mean?' she cried.

Moving away, I opened the blinds on the window a crack. There seemed a few dozen of the bodies milling outside. One noticed me immediately and surged forward into the bars outside the window. His hands flailed at the glass making it shudder in the frame.

'Screw this,' I said. 'Let's go upstairs. It'll be safer and we can see what's happening.'

I helped Summer stand up and we went out into the narrow corridor. Ahead was a circular conference room that we didn't use for much more than the old photocopier that stood in one corner. Round the corner and I put one foot on the stairs and heard a low moaning from the direction of the cell block.

'Shit, I thought I heard something moving back here before,' she said.

'You should have said,' I said, the colour draining out of my face.

Reaching for my baton, I saw it was lost. Empty handed I pushed my nose up to the door leading to the cell block. Through the tiny crisscross wired window in the door the room was dark. A shadow stepped forward and there was a face and teeth slavering at the window. The thing pounded on the door and started crashing wildly into the wood. It took all my strength and to stop it getting in. Small gaps opened, and I saw red, broken fingers reaching round the door. Then it struck me who it was in there; it was Sergeant Dolan.

Dolan was an eighteen stone brute of an officer in life.

'GET HERE AND HELP,' I shouted.

Summer came up beside me and pulled hard on the door but we were tiring within minutes.

'Got an idea,' I said. 'I hold the door and you run and get key eight out of the key box.'

Summer ran back to the office and the thing that had been Dolan went crazy to get in. He was battering at the door and, as if answering his call, every ground floor door and window in the station rattled in their frames under a fierce onslaught. The noise was deafening, and I could barely press the door shut. Sweat ran down inside my uniform in thick rivulets.

'Here it is I think,' she said holding up a red key ring.

It was the key to the firearms store, built into a cupboard under the stairs behind us by eccentric designers. I could have kissed them.

Summer ran and opened the door.

'One, two, three,' I counted and ran with her.

We flung ourselves inside and shut another door. No more than a second later Dolan was pounding to get in too. I pushed the deadbolt into place; we were safe for now.

Summer found the cord and a bare bulb blinked into life. The store was a bit like a Tardis, bigger than the space under the stairs because its length stretched through the side wall and pinched some of the space from the next room along. It smelled musty, with dust sprites dancing in the harsh light.

The door shook but didn't budge. I took solace in the fact that I knew it was reinforced with steel. It was the first time in my life I had ever directed a positive thought at health and safety regulations.

'So what now?' Summer asked. 'Air guns won't stop him.'

I looked too and started sorting through the unruly mess of air weapons, BB guns and air rifles that had been seized and dumped in here over the years.

Shit.

She was right, there was nothing. We would be stuck in here. 'There must be something better,' I said.

At the back of the store, I found an upright pile of sticks. Nearby was an untidy pile of electrical equipment, which was so typical of my colleagues. There was a completely different store for all this, but they just dumped stuff anywhere.

I pushed the sticks out of the way. Finally the prize: a double barrelled shotgun. I checked the exhibit label. It told me it had taken off a suicidal man eighteen months earlier but never reclaimed. Tearing off the plastic cover used to make the weapon safe, one problem remained.

'Summer, where the hell are all the shells?'

We started to turn the place upside down. The pounding kept up on the doors, a remorseless death metal beat.

'Johnny, look,' she said.

We had them, a box of shotgun shells stuffed behind a heap of .22 air gun pellet tins under a desk. I loaded the shotgun and looked over at the door. Sometimes when I'm really nervous about doing something I find it best just to do it; just do it straight away and not even think about it.

I pulled the dead bolt across and the door flung open. Behind me, I heard Summer make an unintelligible sound, like a yowl perhaps.

Dolan lunged, his face grey and his eyes black pools. I pulled on the trigger, instantly deafened by the blast. Dolan flew three feet into a wall and fell down. Cordite smoke choked our lungs and burned our eyes. One of his shoulders was missing, just a red mess of gore and ruined bone. His arm hung off, attached by no more than flimsy, shredded strips of skin. He stirred and went to stand like a god-damn grizzly bear.

'Head shot, Johnny,' Summer said.

Raising the gun, I let him have it. One second his head was there, the next there was nothing but a red geyser and an ugly looking brain stem. My ears rang with an electronic flat line.

'I did it,' I told her.

She slapped me hard across the cheek making me taste blood. 'That's for opening the door without telling me.'

I dropped my eyes, and mimed 'Sorry.' There were dark stains all over her blue uniform. 'I won't do it again,' I told her

Then we heard another voice, deep in the bowels of the station. It came from the cells and I recognized the voice.

'Oh no,' I mumbled.

Re-loading, we edged into Dolan's room. My hand reached behind me and turned on the light switch. Other hands slammed onto the reinforced window outside the station. I looked and could see at least twenty bodies out there looking straight at me, the window glass clear behind the bars.

'It's the light, they're attracted by the light,' she told me and turned it back off.

We crept towards the cell block.

'HELP ME,' the distant voice implored.

The cell block started with a custody desk stuffed full with all manner of bureaucratic forms. Next to the desk were two small holding cells.

'Hey you fucking pigs, I'm bleeding in here,' screamed the voice.

I had arrested the owner of the voice five times in the past five years. I went up to the heavy metal door and pushed back the sliding window panel. Lying on the blue plastic mattress on the raised sleeping platform was Lester Caul, a vagrant who smelled so bad he could make your eyes water. He was a wiry man of forty five, with receded mousey hair and a pair of broken spectacles held together by wire and Sellotape. On a good day he looked like a crazed professor. Often I would find him in the public toilets, a bottle of cheap stolen wine at his feet. He had once managed to set himself on fire and was only saved due to the fact he wore more layers of clothing than skins on an onion, each one of them as brown and soiled as the last.

'I want a doctor and a lawyer, you fucking pig.'

I could see a food tray scattered on the floor of the cell, splashes of blood too. Lester seemed to be cradling his hand like it was injured.

'What's happened, Lester?'

'I'm not speaking with any more fucking biting pigs.'

28

'Did sergeant Dolan bite you, Lester?' Summer asked him.

'For your information yes he did, he did. Wait till my lawyer hears about this,' he slurred.

If I was going to write a statement describing Lester Caul's drunken state I would say things such as his eyes were glassy and he was unsteady on his feet, perhaps adding in he smelt of intoxicating liquor for good luck. The reality was that when Lester was pissed he was a total nightmare to deal with. I knew Dolan was a police officer from the old school and wasn't above throwing drunks into our cells to sober up despite there being a raft of rules to say he couldn't. Dolan had bitten him.

'Listen Lester, we'll get you some help,' I told him, although I doubted if it was the truth.

'We can't just leave him in there,' Summer whispered. 'I'll get the first aid kit.'

She came back with the kit, looked at me nervously. I held the twelve bore in my hands, the grip wet with my sweat.

'If he turns we run and slam this door,' I whispered back. I really didn't want to go in there. I changed my mind.

'Lester, listen to me. We want to help you, believe it or not. Where does it hurt?'

'It fucking hurts where that cock sucker of a police officer bit me. What the fuck is going on? I've never seen so many piss heads on the street before. All I can hear in here is screams and shouts and bangs. What the hell are you people doing?'

'We're not doing anything, Lester,' I said. 'The things out there … we haven't got a clue.'

'Listen, lad,' he said, his voice barely over a whisper. 'Just let me out will you. The booze has gone. I ain't going to do anyone no harm. You know that, don't you?'

'Can't do it, Lester,' I said and took the key off Summer.

'Come on Johnny,' Summer said to me. 'We can't just leave him in there.'

'You've seen those things out there. We can't be sure it's safe. We shouldn't go near anyone we think might be infected. Sod the rules; there's no one else here to help us.'

'Okay, Lester,' I said turning back. 'I'll get you some food and a warm blanket. But you are staying put in there until I know what the fuck is going on.'

I closed the metal slide and muffled the swear words coming my way.

Summer looked at me.

Daggers.

CHAPTER 6

It was dark outside the police station. Peeping around the window blind in the upstairs refreshment room I could see dozens of bodies bumping around in the shady glow of the back car park. They moved stiffly as if fighting off a cramp, resisting the rigor mortis by means unknown.

Summer was sitting, face in her hands. On the table was a CB radio hissing out static. We'd found it in the property store and as far as we could tell it was either broken or nobody used CB radio anymore. We had fiddled and twiddled every switch and dial without the slightest hint of success.

The airwave radio sets, phone lines and mobile phones seemed equally dead. There was no TV in the station and we couldn't find where the old stereo radio was packed away. We felt what we were; cut off from the world we knew and surrounded. I wondered when we were going to wake up.

'I just want to go home,' Summer said again and again.

I knew Summer lived with her parents and sister in a terraced house, ten miles down the country lanes, in a smaller village than Haven, called Wick. My wife had loved the place, and all the dainty tea shops. I wondered what it looked like now.

'Can you wait one night? We'll go in the morning, okay?'

'I don't want to, Johnny.'

'Look, it's late. We're safe here and we should at least try to get some rest. Let's grab some blankets and make up some beds.'

Summer looked a bit dazed and out of it. It was the shock, I figured. I went down to the custody area and grabbed the bedding. Looking in on Lester through the cell door spyhole, I saw he was on his back on the plastic mattress. His skin looked pale and clammy in the torch light, his eye lids flickered as if he was having some sort of vivid dream or nightmare. Part of me wondered what he would be in the morning. Up the stairs, the weariness hit me.

We made our beds up in the inspector's office, as it was the biggest and felt the most secure. The room also had a loft access hatch that we both agreed could be a good escape route if the dead got inside. Summer stayed quiet and went to sleep quickly. I wasn't far behind.

Waking, cold and stiff on the office floor, I didn't know where I was for a second. The moans of the dead brought reality crashing back in. Summer's blanket was empty, and I stared wildly around the room. Flicking the light switch, nothing happened.

I fumbled for the torch on the floor and managed to bang my elbow painfully on the inspector's desk. Had she gone home, left me alone in the world with the drunken vagrant called Lester? The thought was crushing.

I went down the stairs, heard a shout.
'Summer,' I shouted back, running for the cell block, my torch swinging wildly in front of me. I caught the glimpses of the grotesque faces in the windows, and the banging rose up around the station in a wave.

I could hear Lester pounding too from inside the cell door and pulled the metal slide open. Cold terror slipped down my spine when I saw who was inside.

'What the hell are you doing in there,' I said to Summer.

'I'm sorry, I'm so sorry… thought I should check on him,' she said as I shone the torch behind her further into the cell.

'Where is he?' I managed; my mouth dry.

32

'He got out.'

Turning the torch beam, I found him behind me, like a horrible statue.

'Lester?' I said.

He ambled forward.

'Get back,' I tried to shout, but it came out weak.

He loomed over me, Nosfaratu. I drew back my torch to strike the head.

'Lad,' he said. 'You look like you need a drink.'

I started to breathe.

'Johnny,' Summer said from the cell. 'What the fuck is happening and can you let me out? Please? I came down to check on him while you were sleeping and he asked for a drink. I stupidly went in the cell 'cos I couldn't see where he was. He dodged out of the toilet area and shut me in. That was over half an hour ago.'

'Well, that wasn't very nice, Lester,' I said, wary.

He just gave me his stare and shrugged.

Upstairs I found the first aid kit for Lester's arm. Summer set up some candles and Lester sat at the kitchen table and eyed up the CB radio. He was picking at a cold microwave prisoner meal with a custody issue spork.

'I can fix this,' he said.

'Sure you can. We have no power,' I replied.

The man ponged; there was just no getting away from that fact. And the stench rose richer as all five layers of dirty brown upper clothes came away in a heap.

'I'm burning them,' I told him. More staring.

Summer started on the wound, dabbing on cotton wool soaked in antiseptic lotion. She wore clear latex gloves for protection. It looked plain nasty; a tear of flesh obliterating a faded shoulder tattoo of a thorny rose. In the future, it would just be a mess of scars.

The guy didn't even flinch. I guess you don't survive on the streets without the tough streak. I was surprised the booze hadn't killed him off by now.

Lester continued to fiddle with the CB radio, now unscrewing a panel on the back of the set. I watched him intently, knowing I had that twelve bore close at hand. Back to the window, nothing much seemed different out there, but then a new one, a shambling wreck of a fireman. I sighed and turned away, as the CB crackled into life.

'Is anybody getting this?' the radio voice said.

'Loose connection,' Summer explained with a shrug.

'Breaker, breaker,' shouted Lester excitedly. 'Do you fuckers out there have any booze? I'm gagging for a drink!'

'Give me that thing,' I smiled and pulled the transmitter from his hand.

'Fucking eegit.'

'PC Johnny Silverman to last caller. We are three in number at Haven police station. Did you receive last?'

'PC Johnny, we read you alright.'

Saved.

CHAPTER 7

Jack Nation scraped the last dregs of porridge off the side of his bowl. He sat at the head of the kitchen table in the old farmhouse, the house his father had left him and had been in his family for generations. The room temperature was tropical from the Aga stove that sat proud and red against the kitchen wall. Outside, wind rattled at the flaking, white, single pane windows.

5.30am was early for some but not for Jack, who had risen at dawn for as many years as he could remember. He stared blankly out of the window and across his green fields and acres. Lines creased around his eyes like dry bark and his bulbous nose was a light patchwork of red and purple. Relaxed now, he always enjoyed how the tendrils of morning mist danced over the fields, almost playfully inviting him for his day's work. Today was different, he felt, but he couldn't put his finger on why. The feeling sat there in his stomach, heavy as lead. The old Border collie Jess sat watching from the corner of the room, gloomy and subdued. Feel it too, don't you girl, he thought.

'Grand day for the fields, Da,' his oldest son Griffin said from across the table, his lazy eye off at an odd angle.

He didn't reply; he never did.

'Shall I fix up the excavator?' his younger son, Dexter, asked.

He was the younger and the weaker one, the one who stuttered and disappointed him the most. Pale and freckled, ginger hair on top, sometimes Jack wondered if he was even his own child.

'Aye,' he told the pair at last.

They picked up their heavy coats and Wellington boots from the porch. A small part of him was dismayed at leaving another meal's worth of unwashed dishes next to the sink. Plates piled high, with food fused to them like rust on a car. Mostly he didn't care anymore not since his wife Millie had died seven months ago. Heart attack the doctor told him. Of all the things to kill a woman who was as strong as a shire horse, he thought. A woman who could toil from dawn to dusk to make the house shine and put three hot squares on the table every day of the week. She made him go to church too, but he didn't miss that much. Mostly he missed her warm bosom in bed at a night time. He missed the wet purr of her snore, although at the time it had annoyed him no end.

As the three of them trudged over the muddy excrement that filled the farmyard, he remembered finding her. She'd been in out of the house for hours and it had crossed his mind she might have gone into the village on an errand or perhaps to see one of the old dears she sometimes gave a hand with shopping. Then he had seen her car, the little Fiat still parked next to the willow and his old barn. He knew she kept things in the barn, in tea chests up at the top of the loft. With two grown lads in the house, sometimes there just wasn't room for everything amongst the clutter of the house. Wandering in there, he had called out her name. 'Millie. Are you up there?'

When he'd got no reply he had climbed the creaking ladder into the hay loft. In their younger days, he had enjoyed many a young spurt up there, away from the eyes and ears of his own father. Father had been a hard and cruel man but was now long fixed in the earth. At the top of the ladders, he had fully expected to see the floral dress stretched across his wife's wide behind as she bent into one of those boxes for some nic nac or other. Instead, what he saw was his wife lying still on those wooden boards. Her fingers were strained and gripped like claws, as if she was reaching or tearing for something. Looking down, her face had turned purple and unnatural. The back of her bare arms looked black from the pooling of the blood. Her false teeth had slipped out of place to hang out one side of her open mouth. It had made him want to be sick. Punching her on the chest. Hadn't really known what to do. Only a stupid man would know she was far beyond saving. His eyes had stayed dry but inside he had wept ever since. Everyday was empty for him now.

The daydream fell away and he climbed onto the crooked tractor seat. The engine started on the second push of the button with a throaty cough and a plume of dark exhaust smoke. The noise rolled down the valley in a wave. The younger collie dogs ran around the yard excitedly in anticipation of another hard working day.

The hours ticked themselves off as he and his sons ran the ploughs up and down the largest of their fields, cutting long, raw furrows into the earth that would later be ripe for seeds. At lunchtime he felt the familiar sinking feeling that Millie wasn't over there in the distant court yard waving them in. There would be no hot meal waiting, just cold meat sandwiches thick with butter and fatty taste. Up above the farmhouse he could see the tower. He could make out some movement and flashes of red, the tourists up there as usual. Squinting back to his farmhouse a half mile away, he saw something was wrong or out of place. The front door was wide open, and he whistled to his sons like he would call in the dogs and gestured. They set off back, three minds as one. He felt the anger in his veins. The faint bark of Jess told him there was somebody in his house.

Jack marched in through the front door full of purpose with his two sons close at heel.

'Who the fuck is in here? Show yourself.'

He stopped dead at the threshold to the kitchen and just stared. There was man in there with a red waterproof jacket. He must have been middle aged but it was hard to tell for sure. His hair was thin and had an ugly, wet comb-over look. He could be a banker or anybody who liked to wear a suit to work he thought. His skin had an awful grey, waxy look, not like he was just poorly but as if he was mortally ill.

Jack couldn't stop staring at his lips which were all torn and fleshy, teeth that were broken into yellow bladed points. Mainly what made him just stand and stare was the irrefutable fact that this man in red was greedily sinking that disgusting mouth into his beloved dog Jess. The man held the dog's torso high, whilst the poor dog's intestines looped to the floor as if sausages strung in a butcher's window.

'The gun,' he hissed at Griffin.

Griffin turned and eased it down from behind the archway behind, two shakily placed shells into the twin chambers. He handed it back to his father.

What happened next was a blur, as the thing in red dropped the dog and ran at the three of them, causing them to scatter back into the expansive hallway of the farmhouse.

The youngest son tripped over a heavy brass door stop and fell flailing onto his back. The creature fell on top of him and immediately started trying to latch its mouth onto his neck. Dexter pushed down on the creature's shoulders with both his hands, and it took all his strength to hold it no more than a few centimeters from his adrenalin pulsing jugular.

'Get. That. Thing. Off.'

Jack hovered with the gun but couldn't risk the pellets killing his son. He swiveled the twelve bore round and swung the heavy wooden stock at the head of the creature. The sound was akin to cracking open a coconut. Brains splattered a two metre square patch of wallpaper and pooled against the skirting board like lumpy marmalade. The body was still on top of Dexter but looked quite dead now.

'Get it the fuck off me,' Dexter screamed rolling away.

His other son Griffin was already on the phone. *Always the more practical one,* Jack thought.

'It's not working. Phone line is dead.'

Jack checked his own mobile phone. He squinted and saw that the screen on the old brick phone showed no network.

Two more walking corpses trundled in through the open front door. They flung themselves in tandem onto Dexter, who was still not back to his feet. It was as if they sensed he was the weakest target.

The teeth found their mark this time. Dexter's right hand was suddenly missing two fingers and blood was jetting out of the raw wound. Jack got behind the female body who was clawing and biting at Dexter's heavy coat, trying to rip through its stuffing to get at his chest meat. He pulled her backwards and realized her body weight was actually light. He improvised, lifted and swung her entire body in a 180 degree arc until her head collided with a door frame.

Beneath the blonde hair pulled tight in a ponytail, he saw her skull fracture like a broken egg. She went limp and he dropped her.

Dexter was busy with the man who had two of his fingers lodged in his mouth like a pair of bread sticks. He was exhausting himself punching it in the ribs with his free hand whilst the thing tried to latch back onto his ruined mitt.

Jack lurched forward to help, wondering if Griffin had run away, when the same appeared with a large kitchen knife and promptly drove it down to the hilt into the last man's cranium. Griffin gave the knife a turn, the sound was crunching gravel.

'Got to go for the head,' he said breathlessly.

They bandaged Dexter's hand the best they could. He was crying a lot and told them he felt sick and sleepy.

'Griffin, go and get Doc Phillips,' Jack said. 'He's always been good to us. He'll know what to do.'

Griffin took a last worried glance at his brother and went outside. A minute later, the old green Land Rover was heading out the farmyard and up the narrow valley lane to the village.

Jack settled his son into bed and set about pulling the three dead bodies out of the house to lay them side by side in the old barn. He covered them with an old tarpaulin sheet and left them. Back inside the farmhouse he bolted the doors and locked down the windows.

Upstairs his son Dexter sounded like he was talking but he found him still asleep. He figured it must be some awful nightmare he was having because he kept moaning and moving almost in a spasm. Trying to rouse him and feed him some painkillers, he wasn't for waking. He hoped Griffin wouldn't be long.

Two hours later night was down like a black mask and still there was no improvement from Dexter. Jack sat in the kitchen absently turning the dial on the radio. No news, no music, no nothing. He looked at the pattern of red stains around the dog's basket but didn't have the energy to clean it up. He vowed to bury the dog later. The younger dogs barked out in the court yard, but he didn't care about them.

Later, when the electric lights went out he wasn't entirely surprised. Jack pulled on his Wellingtons again and stepped out into the dark yard with his torch. Cold mist was on his breath and the rutted mud on the ground had taken on ice and was hard underfoot. The smaller building next to the barn housed his diesel generator. Jack thought it slightly odd that all his dogs had stopped barking. Whistling, none would come to heel. Looking around cautiously, he couldn't catch any movement in the fields with his torch beam.

Jack walked across his farmyard, every other foot crunching on small frozen puddles between the ruts. The cold breeze rustled over the fields and seeped into his clothes. The generator house looked a little like a garage with paneled wooden door set in cream pebble-dashed walls. His father had built it in a time when power cuts had been more common, and out of respect for him, he'd always maintained it. Jack fiddled with the twenty plus keys he had on his key ring before finding the small Yale key that would fit the lock.

There was a noise of falling rock from behind him. Turning, he flashed the torch to its source. Two or more bodies were awkwardly throwing themselves over the dry stone wall that lined the perimeter of the farmhouse. Low moans filled the air. Caught in a fight or flight blood rush, he hesitated and then fumbled at the door lock to the generator room. The lock turned and he grabbed the handle and turned it. Already the first body had reached him and Jack kicked out wildly catching its knee with a crack. The teenager fell, taking a tear of Jack's waterproof coat in his teeth to the frozen ground.

Jack didn't waste time. Inside the generator building, he shut the door behind him. At least two other of the creatures started hammering on the wooden door to get inside. He dropped his keys and scrabbled around desperately to retrieve them. The things outside were too stupid to turn a door handle otherwise he'd have been in serious trouble. Jack moved down the musty corridor and let his hands play over the massive diesel generator controls. He found the hand pulley and to his relief it roared into life after a single yank. Life was illuminated again and he was bathed in neon light from the strips on the ceiling. In a dusty deck chair, he waited, as the creatures thumped and scratched a steady beat on his door.

His watch read 1am when he heard a familiar diesel sound coming down the lane. He heard the vehicle hiss into the courtyard, skid and grind to a stop. Griffin's voice was shouting, and then the sharp repeat of the shotgun twice and then twice again. Stray pelts clattered and chipped into the outside wall of the generator room.

'Da, are you in there?'

The door of the generator room opened and for a moment Jack found himself staring into the barrel of Griffin's raised shotgun.

'Yes son, I'm fine. What took you so long?'

Jack looked around and counted four fresh cadavers decorating his farmyard. All four had the grey look and heads that were no longer fully part of their bodies. Griffin was a good shot.

'Da it's totally crazy out there. These things are everywhere. I tried the Doc's house and he was there alright, but with bits of his wife in his teeth. I went further Da, all the way to Havelock. It was a nightmare, wrecked cars with things wriggling inside. It got so blocked I took to the fields, but even then the things were everywhere. I got spooked by one and ended up getting the Land Rover stuck in the mud. I thought I was a goner right there. It took me hours to get moving and it was pitch black. I just thought I should get back. Good job I did, I think.'

Jack shone his torch over at the Land Rover noting the fresh mud and dents it had picked up. Then he saw somebody sat in the passenger seat, her face white as a ghost.

'And Da, I found this woman up at the tower. She was stuck up the steps waving her red coat at me. I think her husband turned into one of those things we killed. She's freezing.'

Jack smiled over to her and waved.

42

'Griffin, get her inside and get her some warm food. I need to check on your brother.'

Jack marched back inside the house suddenly worried. He went up to Dexter's room and flung open the door. Dexter still appeared to be asleep. His temperature was high and his skin had a sickly shine of sweat.

'Dexter, are you awake?' he said softly.

Dexter didn't reply and he decided it best to leave him until the morning. If anything, he thought he looked slightly better. He went over to his bedroom and gathered some clothes from a drawer he hadn't been in for a long time. Millie's clothes. They smelt bad but he didn't expect the woman would mind.

He went downstairs and found his son stoking the stove back into life. The woman sat at the table and looked in a state of shock. Her red coat was covered with dirt.

'You need to get those things off,' he said placing the clothes on to the table. 'What's your name love?

'Alison,' she replied looking up at him. 'Where am I, please?'

'You're at The Old Lodge. But you're fine now. You're going to be safe here.'

'Do you know what's happened?' Alison said.

'Not really love. My best case is those terrorists have released something. Or maybe it's the government, some experiment that's gone pear shaped. I don't know. All I do know is there are dead things out there that should be under dirt and under ground. If I see them, that's where I'll be putting them.'

'Here's your coffee and there's hot soup on the way,' Griffin said.

'Thank you,' she said and smiled for the first time.

'I'll run you a hot bath,' Jack said eventually.

It had been a while since they'd had a woman in the house. Not since Millie had died in fact, discounting his

43

sister and the district nurse. He felt a little tongue tied and unsure of himself. Would Millie have approved of him taking this woman in? Of course she would have. She'd always been the charitable sort in life. Jack ran the bath and found his best towel.

Later, when he lay in bed, he thought of her in the bath and he thought about how this world had turned out in the end. Out of bed, he creaked along the narrow corridor to the spare bedroom. Downstairs he could hear Griffin talking into his old CB radio. Near the spare bedroom door, his heart danced like a sixteen year old boy's again.

'Is everything okay?' she asked.

'Listen, I've been thinking. We all need to earn our keep now.'

He let his dressing gown slide to the floor.

CHAPTER 8

'I think we should meet. Over.'

There was a long pause.

'Yes. Okay, PC Silverman we agree. Over.'

'What is your name? I don't think we've met. Over.'

'Griffin Nation.'

By the time dawn came, none of us had had any sleep. We'd agreed on the CB to try and meet at the local Women's Institute building later in the day. The building had strong doors and windows and a good location on the edge of the village. We hoped it might be relatively free of the bodies. I also had a spare set of keys for the WI hung up in the police station.

Summer and I stood bleary eyed around the gas hob in the kitchen watching water boil in a pan. Behind us Lester sat grumbling about some great injustice or other and eating a hearty portion of stale cereal from the cupboard. Police station cupboards accumulated unwanted food, often left for years. Lester had no misgivings about the combination of blueberry and mango crunch.

'We'll take the 4x4. It's the most powerful vehicle and can handle the off-road driving if we run into any road blocks.

'Okay I suppose,' Summer said. 'But I'm not going to any stupid community meeting until we've gone to my parent's house and checked they're okay. I can't leave it any longer Johnny, I'm going nuts.'

I quietly opened the back door of the police station while Summer, and to a lesser extent Lester, acted as lookouts through the drying room window. There were seven bodies in the main car park but I was mindful that others could be hidden behind corners and walls around the outside of the police station.

Removing my fluorescent jacket, I just kept on my black police fleece. My handcuffs and incapacitant spray were redundant. I carried the twelve bore in one hand and the key fob to the 4x4 in the other.

I made my dash for the driver door, timing it for when I felt all seven bodies were facing away from me. The closest one looked young and was staggering around in an old Guns and Roses t-shirt, no more than ten metres away. The 4x4 lights all flashed at once and with a dull clunk, the central locking released.

Tricky part next. I beckoned to Summer and Lester in the window to come out and follow me. Keeping my head ducked down, I was mindful to keep out of sight.

Summer ran out of the door and flung herself into the passenger seat. Her eyes looked wild and her cheeks burning red.

'He's not coming,' she managed.

'What?'

'He said he may be a fucking drunk but he's not fucking drunk enough to do anything this stupid.'

'Fair to say he's sobered up,' I said.

'Not for long I bet. Come on, let's get going.'

I started the engine, paused and then crept the 4x4 forward. Despite the stealth, it didn't take long for the dead to turn our way. They flocked at the vehicle like demented flamingos. Pressing the accelerator, we lurched forward just as the Guns and Roses man had his fingertips on my driver window. Turning hard onto Main Street I left the police station behind. Summer looked across and gave me a tense smile. We were lost together in this dead new world.

Dropping down we passed the local pub, The Archer, on the corner. My eyes were fixed on the road but my peripheral vision featured bodies scattered and pacing all over the expansive beer garden. The road ran parallel to the beach and estuary, and I saw a red sign warning of quicksand flash by. To my right ran a line of the village shops, a bakery, a gift shop, a butcher's and the village's other general store. Windows looked broken and there were bodies inside and out. I spotted the woman who used to sell me meat pies and cakes shambling across the road, a bloody Rorscharch stain on her apron. To my left I could see the railway bridge stretching the miles across the sands and tidal waters of the bay.

The road narrowed as we approached our railway station, and I slowed to ten mph as more bodies littered the tarmac. No way was I going to stop and I deliberately clipped one man and then another with the bull bars at the front of the 4x4. The second body flew six feet and marked the windscreen and bonnet of a parked car. On the pavement, I could see the disturbing sight of a dead man pulling his dog behind him, the animal clearly aware its master was now an unnatural and dangerous thing. It pulled and rolled wildly on its lead to get away, but was dragged on towards the village.

We bore left under the railway bridge and I accelerated out of the village. Four miles later, we faced the choice of risking a single track lane or joining the motorway for a much longer stretch.

'We can't risk the country road being blocked. I'd have to reverse or risk a difficult manoeuvre to turn around. They could be on us in that time. I think we have to go down,' I said, looking from our position on the motorway bridge.

Below us I could see cars and lorries parked and crashed all over the three lanes. 'Yeah okay. The hard shoulder looks clear,' Summer said, 'and we can use the 4x4 on the banking at the side to get round any bad blocks.'

I engaged the gear and we headed down the slip road with care, constantly having to weave a path through the parked metal. We went straight onto the rouge banded hard shoulder.

'I can see them moving in the cars,' Summer told me. 'They're pawing at the windows. They're dead; they're all dead in there, Johnny.'

'I know,' I replied.

I was more worried about the ones out of the cars. The ones that kept drifting through gaps in the cars and that I could see in my rear view mirror filling the space on the hard shoulder where they'd just been. It was a blessing these ones were slow to react, otherwise we'd really be in trouble.

Twice we had to ride the banking with the 4x4 tyres straining and tearing at the turf to get around first a badly parked car and then a coach toppled onto its side. Glass shards were everywhere and I wondered what we'd do if we got a puncture. Finally, I saw the sliproad off the next juncture and we were free of the carnage and back on a wide country road towards the village of Wick.

'We're nearly there,' she said.

I could only imagine how she was feeling. I thought about my wife again, the dark cloud of guilt. I needed to think clearly and stay on track. People were counting on me it seemed, but it didn't stop the screaming emptiness building inside.

Summer's house was an average sized three bedroom mid terrace off a short cul-de-sac. I parked the Freelander in the middle of the road and purposefully left the engine running. The gauge on the dashboard told me we only had half a tank of fuel left. *Just another problem for later,* I thought.

'Have you got your key?' I asked.

'You know you can wait here if you want. I'll be okay.'

'You're kidding right?' I said. 'I wouldn't let you go anywhere that dangerous on your own.'

'Do you think they are going to be alright?'

I paused and her face dropped.

'You should take this,' I told her.

'Okay.'

Summer got out of the 4x4 with a small but very sharp hatchet in her hand. I followed behind with the shotgun looking out for movement on the street. There was none. Summer took out her key and pushed it into the lock. She took a large breath and turned the door handle.

The hallway carpet had an old fashioned tortoiseshell look which reminded me of my grandmother's old house. We edged our way down, intently listening for any movement. Ahead of us were stairs leading up to the three second floor bedrooms. At the bottom of the stairs was a door on the right hand side which led into a through lounge diner, a kitchen and a downstairs bathroom.

Summer pushed open the door and stepped into the dining area. I followed her and immediately it was clear that we had a problem. The mess was considerable. Broken crockery and food strewn throughout the three rooms. In the dining room, the table had at least two legs shattered as if somebody's full weight had fallen on top of it at some point. It was clear to me whatever had happened to Summer's parents and sister may not turn out to be pretty.

'They'll be okay,' she mumbled.

'We should search the rooms. Carefully,' I said.

I took the lead and edged up the two short steps out of the end of the kitchen to the bathroom door. I pressed my ear as close as I dared to the door and listened for any tell-tale movements. I looked at Summer and saw how wide her eyes had become, somewhere between terror and hysteria.

'It's going to be okay,' I whispered.

Someone or something must have heard me; something rustled inside the room. I paused but Summer went straight ahead and opened the bathroom door. At first it didn't look like anyone was there but then it was clear somebody was lying in the bath. We walked in and I raised the gun.

In the bath was a young woman in her late teens. She was slumped on her back half covered in a shower curtain that had been ripped violently from its hooks. Her body had the waxy, doll-like look I'd had seen before at countless sudden deaths. She wasn't moving and she appeared dead. The sound had come from a small ginger cat on her chest. Red tears in her shoulder where it had recently eaten. Trapped and starving it had had no choice.

'I'm so sorry,' I said.

Summer just stood, unmoving, I went to touch her and move her out of the room. She felt stiff and rigid.

'We can't just leave her there,' she sobbed.

'Don't worry, Summer we ...' I started to say but the movement above stopped me. 'Oh no,' I finished.

Summer was already out of the dining room door and running up the stairs. I ran after her as she made straight for the master bedroom at the end of the corridor. She opened the door and then slammed it shut again. In that second it was clear to see that there were two bodies in that room, a male and a female of an age that must make them Summer's parents. Their hands started to pound on the door.

'I've lost everything,' she said

'Well, you haven't lost me.'

We started moving away from the room and back down the stairs. We got as far as the front door when she turned to me.

'I need to do something,' she said.

'We need to leave, Summer. We need to go now.'

50

'Just go to the car, Johnny. Just go and it will okay. I won't be long.'

She turned and went back to the stairs. I watched her go but somehow I knew better than to follow her. It crossed my mind that maybe she just wanted to end it all, and that the despair was too much to live with. I didn't know how I felt when I turned to the front door and walked outside.

Already I could see three bodies down the street, but thankfully not close. I got into the driver's seat and waited. I doubted I would have the courage to go back outside if Summer didn't appear. How much horror can one person take before the mind distorts and shatters? Part of me wondered how long I would wait before I would set off and drive back alone.

Summer opened the passenger door. I hadn't even noticed her leave the house. Her skin was pale and she looked like a ghost. There was blood all the way up her slender arms and the hatchet looked blood wet.

'I couldn't just leave them like that.'

'What about the cat?'

'Fuck the cat.'

CHAPTER 9

Lester watched the two of them drive away in their bright liveried police car. He didn't necessarily think he'd see them again given the current issue with dead people walking the streets, and on reflection he wasn't convinced he cared a whole heap either. In his experience of living rough on the street people always came and went, and there would always be new ones to take their place. A couple of quid bottle of the cheap stuff was Lester's best friend anyway.

Smacking his lips together, his tongue felt like an old bit of leather lolling around his gob. Possibly, it might be rotting in there. Every month some part of his body seemed more flayed around the edges. Sticking his tongue out in the mirror, it looked a nasty shade of purple. Purple was never a good colour, Lester thought.

Standing in a room full of stinking policemen's kit bags, it tickled him to think most of them would be shambling around out there on the streets like the worst kind of Jakie, the kind they used to throw in a van and a cell for opening their mouths and speaking their minds. He knew what it was like to be arrested for every offence the lawmen had ever thought up, and wait out the hours in the cupboard sized cells watching the shakes come on. When an honest man couldn't piss on a war memorial, whilst necking a tinny and strumming 'I am a walrus' on a three stringed guitar you knew the world was fucked. Having a few dead bodies turn up in a pissed off mood was just the cherry on the top of a particularly fucked up cake.

He really needed a drink!

He started by fumbling through a few of the bags, but they all seemed the have the same useless police junk inside and not even the hint of a silver hip flask or a little whisky bottle. *Did these people not drink at work anymore?*

He wandered into their office room with all the computers, all so dead and useless now. He needed to think, but one of the bodies started hitting a dirty palm on the thickened glass of one of the frosted windows.

'Shut up you goon! Some of us have brains and are trying to think in here.'

Lester paced around in tight circles muttering and repeating things to himself. He remembered there was nothing in the kitchen or he would have seen it already. The other rooms looked too empty and tidy. He knew he was missing something, something really obvious.

That was it, Lester thought. *The bastards go after the children as well.*

He started looking for a key, rustling through all the files and useless bits of paper that were in the pigeon holes on the wall. Soon it was all an untidy heap on the floor. Not a single key. Carrying on, Lester first ransacked a corner cupboard and then a shelving unit designed for external post.

At last success; a small box drilled into place on the wall. He flipped open the cover and found rows of shiny silver and copper keys. He figured one of them must open a place where they stashed all the booze they snatched from the children. Lester had seen it many a time on the streets on the weekends. The bastards had nothing better to do than jump on poor kids just trying to have a few ales after a miserable week at school. Lester would always share his grog with them, well the ones who didn't curse him and set him on fire when he slept anyway.

Now which key? He read off some labels.

'Front door, back door, electrical store, misc store, interview room, garage.'

No reference to booze or kids.

'Houston, we have a problem.'

Standing, he kicked the paper pile in disgust.

The garage. It's got to be that garage.

Eyeing the bodies again from the drying room window, he counted off five of the damn things. Not having the constant babble of the pig and his blonde pig assistant must have meant a few had lost interest. He liked his chances.

Opening the back door a sneak he looked out. It smelled rank out there. Four of the bodies were being nicely distracted in the car park by the squawk of a large crow prancing on the roofs of cars. The other one was an old woman who was wandering off in a random diagonal, away from the station.

Back into the drying room, he grabbed a large dragon light torch off its charger.

Smart one Lester.

Lester stepped out and paced quickly to the back door of the garage. He looked down at the lock and looked at the keys in his hand. Only then did he realise there were at least three other keys on the same key ring and they were all different shapes. He heard a flutter and squawk as the crow buggered off. Lester looked over his shoulder and saw more than one set of dead eyes looking his way.

The first key went half way into the lock and then got stuck. It was clearly too big and Lester had to wrench it back out. Looking to the bodies again, he saw them closing fast. The next key stabbed at the lock and it wouldn't go in at all.

'Fuck you!'

There were two dead young men ten metres away where the police cars parked. Their faces were purple all over. Escape back into the police station was cut off. To his left he heard a scratching, hissing sound which he knew must be one or more of those things dragging themselves

54

down the alley next to the garage. He was getting surrounded.

The third key. And it turned. Pushing the door, it opened it with a jolt. Lester shut it again in time to see a young, dead face leer up into the toughened, wire crossed glass and head butt it with a wet *thud*. Already the bodies at the front were beating on the roller shutter door at the far end of the garage. Lester stood there in the dark and tried to be quiet, but they knew he was in there and wouldn't shut up.

'Fuck you all! Now where's that booze?'

He went into the dusty murk, instantly tipping over a pedal cycle balanced against at least a dozen more. They clattered over like dominoes and Lester reached forward and felt a bruised lump rising on his left shin.

'CUNTY BASTARDS!'

He counted at least six dead faces straining for a look in the back door window, and more behind them.

I've seen more brain power in a midget's rod end.

He stood and started to search for the light switch. His hands traced a cobweb trail along the garage wall before he remembered the dragon light and the fact that all the power was out. He found it under the heap of bikes and flicked it on. The beam cut through the dank air and illuminated a whole array of non-booze related items including *'useless prick licking'* police cones, a *'fucking fascist'* speed monitoring device, more bikes and miniature motorbikes with engines. Then his foot kicked a plastic box that sounded full of glass bottles. He reached down and found empty jam jars and a post-it note that read *'for re-cycling.'*

This was getting dire. In one front corner of the garage he could see the purple fingers reaching under the gap beneath the roller shutter. He went over and stamped on them with the heel of his boot, grinding them down into the concrete floor like mashed worms.

'Teach you motherfuckers!'

He took a step back when the fingers returned; broken white sticks of bone, but still scratching the dirt and reaching for him.

Lester was puzzled for ideas for a moment before he struck gold. The holy grail was before him on a shelf behind a chest freezer; eight tins of Foster's lager and a nasty coloured Bacardi Breezer. A tinny was downed in seconds with the slick skill of an alcoholic pro. Lester could set records for downing first pints. Can two was on his crusty lips before he'd even bothered to take breath, draining down like a dynamite plunger.

That felt right and that felt like justice. 'Fuck you creeps,' he cried.

He gathered the rest of the booze into a cardboard box and picked it up with both hands. The bodies were still crowding around the back door but Lester had a plan. He turned the key on the back door and let them flow in just as the mini-moto at the bottom of the garage burst into flames. Lester had lit a rag fuse into the fuel tank a few seconds earlier. The bodies surged at the bright flames as thick acrid smoke filled the garage.

Lester nimbly stepped from behind the door and tottered into the courtyard. Black smoke billowed up behind him like an industrial chimney.

'Houston, you're not going to like this,' he said.

The back door of the police station was wide open, things moving inside.

CHAPTER 10

The Woman's Institute had been a part of the village since the 1950's. It was a meeting place for numerous strange meetings and societies, coffee mornings, jumble sales and assorted what-the-hells. It had been a church once, and so was built with thick stone walls and reinforced buttresses. The institute sat on raised ground on the edge of the village, far away from the shops and houses. There was a small but neat ornamental garden and lawn, popular with the women's croquet club in brief summer months.

I parked the 4x4 badly as always, near an unattended green Land Rover I guessed belonged to Griffin, the farmer on the CB radio. There were other cars clustered near, bringing with it the hope there may be far more living people than Summer and I had imagined. We'd had a rough journey back along the motorway, with the dead things making a concerted effort to get at our vehicle. We'd spent the seven mile stretch mostly on the banking as the hard shoulder was packed tightly with the dead. It was as if they remembered us, but to look at their cold, lifeless masks it was hard to imagine thought even entered into it.

'Look how many people are here,' Summer said, excited. 'Who would have thought so many people had survived?'

We grabbed our weapons and got out to join the party. At the entrance were two men, both clearly related in the local in-bred way. The older man had a weathered look about him, as if his face was sandblasted every morning before breakfast. The lines on his face looked black, where dirt hid never to be found.

'Jack Nation,' he said offering a callused hand. 'And this is Griffin.'

I looked at the younger man warily. He looked the same age as myself but broader. One eye looked a little funny and off-centre, spoiling his looks. He looked a bit bitter about it. His whole demeanour screamed *watch out*.

'Hi, Jack and Griffin. I'm PC Johnny Silverman and this is your local friendly PCSO Summer Harris.'

'That's a funny name,' Jack said.

'What can I say? My parents were the hippy types,' Summer shrugged.

Summer was looking a little tearful again. 'I think we should move this inside,' I said.

I kept checking the road behind us for the moving dead, but it was clear. Jack was looking at me with a weird squint in his eyes. Anti-police? If he didn't like the uniform, I could sense problems down the road for us all.

'Okay, let's get inside,' Jack said. 'Griffin has done amazing work rounding some of these people up and getting them here. Others wouldn't leave their houses, too scared, but this is a great turn out. Look at them all.'

And I did. On the folding chairs in front of the stage, I counted at least thirty five healthy people. It was a fantastic feeling not to be alone anymore. Under different circumstances, I could have imagined this was a perfectly normal WI event, perhaps one of the old dears back from their hols with a riveting slideshow.

Only the sombre mood gave it away. People were down-faced and some ill looking. Most were sipping hot drinks from white polystyrene cups. There was an atmosphere in the hall not unlike a wake. I could see various, perhaps fractured family groups clustered on the chairs, often with gaps between sad, lonely looking old men and woman. Haven was after all predominantly a retirement village, a place where the old went to enjoy the scenery and the quiet life, and generally not be menaced by the dead trying to bite their faces off for fun.

I recognised some of them by name from my foot patrols and the interminable parish council meetings. Meetings I did my best to avoid, but that always found me in the end. In particular, I could see that the Hanson family were there in an intact state. Toby Hanson and his pregnant wife Jean and their two eleven and twelve year old sons Mark and Phillip. I knew those two well enough due to their fondness for breaking and burning random street furniture around the village. I'd personally interviewed both for arson of four waste paper bins and knew they'd received every police slap on the wrist possible, short of youth court in their time. They looked happy enough sat with their mum and dad. I think they thought this was one big harmless adventure.

'Do you have any news?' a hunched old man said.

'No, not really,' I mumbled as heads began to turn, and the murmur of voices rose a notch.

Looking at those expectant faces, it finally dawned on me how much these people would be looking up to me to have answers, and to lead them in some way. I felt my hands go clammy just at the thought. I'd never been what you could describe a career mover or shaker. I had no ambitions to be a sergeant or a detective, and in all honesty my overriding thought when at work was always, 'How long till I finish?' I could see now my attitude needed adjustment.

'Why don't you go up on the stage and tell them what you know,' I heard Jack say loudly.

I caught that glint in his eye again. It was as if he was probing for my soft spot and wanted me to feel as uncomfortable as possible. I'd always hated public speaking all the way through school. The fear had diminished in this job but the fact remained I was a rubbish orator at the best of times. Taking a gulp of air, I wandered to the stage. In the end I just leaned against it rather than standing so high above everyone. Summer followed me, but then sat down at the front, lost in grief.

'Hi. A lot of you may already know me, but for those that don't I'm a police officer at Haven Police Station, Johnny Silverman.'

The brothers, Phillip and Mark were giggling, and the faces in front of me were looking blank. Already not going well.

'Like you, I'm as mystified as you as to what's gone on today. From my point of view, it seemed a completely normal day. I did find a dead seal and some chemicals on the beach, but that could have been anything. We all know how much rubbish and debris gets washed up on there, week in, week out. I went from the beach to Tomlinson's, and suddenly it was like all hell had broken out. I can't say how or why all this has happened, but I promise I will do my best to find out.'

'Have you heard from anyone outside the village on those fancy police radios?' Griffin shouted out.

'No, I haven't. Nothing since this morning. After the supermarket incident the radios went down completely. I can only imagine that there has been a power failure at one of the local airwave radio masts and it knocked us all off the air. The last things I heard on the radio, I have to say, were not good. It would seem to confirm that what has happened here is widespread, that it could be everywhere.'

'You're not joking it's widespread. I went to town and the whole place is fucking over-run with those things,' shouted Griffin excitedly.

'I don't think we need to be scaring anyone Griffin,' I said looking at the poor old dears' faces. Griffin just stared back.

'I think it's gone a little beyond sparing people's feelings, Officer,' Jack said. 'Everyone in this room has seen first hand what's out there and what they do. Those fuckers

60

bit my son Dexter and he's in a terrible state. I don't know if he'll pull through. Let's not beat around anyone's bush. Some of these good folk tell me their own loved ones died, rose up and tried to kill them. The dead have come out to play and they're hankering to eat every last one of us.'

'So what do we do, Officer?' asked a man in his thirties sat with his wife or girlfriend.

'I think we wait. We find our safe places in this village and we wait it out. I think the army and the government will come good eventually but until that time comes, we have to stay warm, dry and feed ourselves. We need to arm ourselves and fight those things if we have to.'

'Hit 'em hard enough about the head and they go down like a sack of shit. Just like the movies, Johnny. Maybe we could show zombie films in here and educate the old folks,' Griffin said, beaming.

'No, I don't think that would be appropriate. And that reminds me, the power has gone down. I know some of you have your generators, but we have great wind generators on the hills that bring a lot of our power. Does anyone know why they would have stopped working?'

'My name's Bob Sack,' said a portly man two rows back. 'I can only think it's the dead creatures. They could have gotten into the maintenance rooms and caused havoc. I don't know how precisely they go together, but I am a trained electric maintenance engineer and may be able to do something to help. Just give me the nod and I'll go up there with you.'

'That's an excellent idea. If we are going to sit this out comfortably we are going to need that electricity,' I said.

'I've got an even better idea,' said Jack. 'We all know we're not safe in the village anymore with those biters running around wild. I want us all to build a fence and keep those bastards out. I've got enough high tensile fencing back on the farm to fence a distance of three thousand feet at least. We get it up and we get it up fast. Reinforce the posts and kill every biter left inside. Then you have yourself one safe village Officer Silverman.'

'Sounds better and better. How long will that take us?'

'What, you want maybe I quote you the job, Johnny?' he said when he was interrupted by a banging on the door.

'Go see who it is Griffin,' Jack said.

There was a hushed silence in the group as Griffin pulled open the door and ushered an elderly man inside. He looked off-colour and sick, and he kept bringing a stained handkerchief up to his mouth between racking coughs. I half recognised him but couldn't put a name to the craggy face. People were already on their feet and shying away from him.

'What do you think,' Jack shouted out, 'is he gonna turn biter on us?'

Griffin took hold of the old man's arms as he bent over to cough again. Griffin looked to me like he was trying to sniff the guy. Like that was going to tell him anything. Jack was walking over towards them looking purposeful. I pushed off from leaning on the stage. I'd seen enough confrontation scenes kick off in my six years as a police officer to sense something bad was about to happen.

'Are you holding him tight?' Jack shouted over to Griffin.

The other villagers had moved into both corners at the opposite end of the hall. The Hanson parents were trying to shield Mark and Phillip from what was going on but they were determined to see and kept pulling away to look. Some of the older men were edging closer and offering to help Griffin.

'Look guys,' I said, starting to walk over. 'I've seen this bloke, he's always looking ill. It's normal for him.'

'He doesn't look very normal to me,' said Jack. 'He looks like he wants to turn into something that likes to use his teeth.'

I could see the old man clearly. He was bent over and coughing, hawking up bloody phlegm. His skin did look very grey, but I considered that might be normal for someone of his advanced age. His eyes were bloodshot. The old man started to shake his head, but the movement looked odd and unnatural. More like a spasm than an attempt to communicate.

'Can you hear me down there old fella? Is there anything we can do to help you? Are you feeling okay?' I said looking down on him.

'I really don't think he's listening,' said Griffin, visibly beginning to struggle with the old man, despite holding his arms pinned back.

'Look at him officer, he's starting to turn,' Jack shouted across to me.

'Listen Johnny, Jack's right,' Summer said, appearing next to me. 'We need to do something with him. He's going to get dangerous.'

Looking around the hall, I saw many fearful eyes. They wanted me to make a decision, but I just wasn't sure.

'Look, I think maybe he's just sick,' I said again.

The old man's pupils were starting to take on a hint of jaundiced yellow. There was a snarl coming over his mouth and I could see that this guy still held his own teeth. They looked black with unchecked plaque and decay. I had called this all wrong.

The old man was writhing and thrashing as Griffin held back his wrists. The sounds out of the man's mouth were both animal and guttural. I could hear his old bones grind and crack as he threw his body into awful shapes. He was trying to bite out at Griffin.

'Hold him still will you, Griffin?' Jack shouted.

I stood with the other men, too rooted and scared to take a step forward and risk a stray bite.

Jack took something resembling a heavy metal cosh out his pocket and rapped it twice on the old man's skull. On the second impact, it seemed to go inside the old man's head like rock breaking through ice. Griffin let the old man's body fall where blood pumped and pooled over the varnished wooden floor.

'Jesus Christ,' I said and looked away.

'It's okay, he's dead now. He can't hurt anyone,' Jack said to the people in the corners.

I felt Summer take told of my arm and cling on. She guided me away and back towards the stage.

Sometime later, when the body had been covered and the sobbing had died away, we made our plans. Bob Sack was coming with us, and we apparently were going to bring power back to this godforsaken place.

CHAPTER 11

Summer and I were the last to drive away from the WI. Bob Sack told us he had to go home first for some tools, and would meet us at agreed point near the wind farm in an hour or so. We'd spent the last half hour helping ferry the rest of the scared survivors back to their vehicles so they could drive away safely. Three more times zombies had stumbled into view and three times Griffin had put them down before I'd even had a chance to react. Blood thirty.

Summer looked like she was worried. 'Are you sure this is a good idea? None of us knows anything about wind farms really. Bob looks like a fat idiot.'

'I think we've got to give it a shot. Hardly anyone said they had a generator and winter is nearly on us.'

'Well, I suppose we do have that woman who is pregnant to consider.'

'You what?' I said puzzled. 'Oh yes, Jean Hanson.'

'It's due in a couple of months. Why do you think she looked so worried? I haven't got a clue what to do, and Griffin said the village doctor is dead.'

'I don't know. We'll have to read a book or something. How hard can it be?' I said with false bravado.

'Well, we've got to get the power back on. Worry about Jean Hanson when we have too.'

We'd driven back to the police station to freshen up and collect Lester. What we didn't expect to see was the garage attached to the station reduced to blackened, skeletal cinders. Tendrils of dark smoke floating up to the heavens. We drove around to the car park at the back, and there amongst the parked panda cars Lester stood waving a large public order baton in one hand and a tin of lager in the other. Swinging for the head of a burning man crawling towards him, too drunk to aim, he kept missing and overbalancing. The zombie's face was burnt like the underside of a barbequed hamburger. Lester finally found the target, the baton disappearing into the man's face, showing the pink tenderised cooked flesh beneath the blackened skin. The burnt man collapsed and lay still.

More charred bodies crawled and slithered in the remains of the garage, one so fried only its white teeth distinguished it from the burned up debris. The garage was finished, but thankfully, the side wall and the roof to the police station hadn't set on fire. The thick, caustic smell reminded me of the burning pyres of cows and sheep built by the farmers during the foot and mouth crisis years before. Running my eyes over the police station, it still appeared structurally sound. It would still be able to keep us safe.

'Lester, what the hell have you been playing at?'

'You ungrateful fucker,' he said. 'Can't you see all the good work I've done for you here?'

'Lester you've nearly burnt the place down, you crazy bastard.'

'I won't try and dispute your fascist facts Officer, but I killed plenty of those fuckers. You go and see.'

It was then I saw that the back door to the police station was ajar. *Better and better.*

'Come on,' said Summer holding her hatchet again. 'Let's go and see what he's left us.'

'Wait up,' I shouted, trying to keep up with Summer. The girl was fearless.

Lester had certainly left his mark on the place. The drying room was in chaos with over a dozen bags lying torn open and their contents strewn across the floor. In the report room, it got worse with crushed and empty lager cans covering desks and crumpled, trodden down paperwork everywhere. It was hard to miss the bloodstains, like multiple red snail trails leading out of the door and into the adjoining room used for photocopying and occasional meetings.

Inside there it was like an abattoir with blood thick and congealed on the harsh, bristled, auburn carpet. I counted five bodies in there with a wide variety of severe blunt force traumas to their craniums. One unfortunate old woman appeared to have a fist full of biro pens lodged squarely through one eye. It evidently hadn't been enough to cease all function as her other eye rotated wildly like a loose marble. Lester appeared next to me and said, 'Did I miss you, dear?' Then he bashed the pens all the way in with what looked like an old croquet mallet.

'Found it in a bush,' he slurred.

'Perhaps we should put you back in the cell.'

Lester gripped a little harder on the mallet and was clearly less than keen.

'No, don't worry Lester, nobody is locking you up,' Summer said and looked hard at me. 'It was probably our fault for leaving you behind.'

She went on to explain at length all the events from the Women's Institute and how many had survived and were also hiding in the village. I saw Lester visibly relax and become less belligerent. It was a truism in the police service that although men in the main were the physically superior in a confrontation situation, it was often female officers who could calm the heat out of a conflict and resolve things without brute force being needed. Although Summer was only a PCSO she seemingly possessed all the feminine wiles to twist Lester around her little finger.

'We are going up to the wind farm Lester to try and get the power back on. I want you to come with us and help us. Is that okay?' she finished.

'Yes that is fine. Just remember I'm doing it because you have a lovely smile and not because your fascist friend is threatening to lock me up again.'

'Okay, Lester,' I said. 'Truce.'

We teased Lester into the back seat of the 4x4 and set off again. Summer produced sandwiches from her bag as if by magic, but in fact, she said that she'd been handed them at the Woman's Institute by a kindly old dear. We ate the food greedily, all three of us ravenous, having lived off the fumes of adrenalin for the best part of twenty four hours.

I steered a course that would parallel to a certain extent the route we'd taken to Summer's parents' house. The high tide was up on the foreshore of the beach. The frothing water lapped over the coarse sand grasses and footpaths that ran below the sea wall. We again passed the row of local shops, noting human activity amongst the stumbling dead. Griffin and other men from the Institute were looting the butcher's shop. They had the old green Land Rover on the pavement and nearly inside the entrance. White plastic bags and, what I took to be fresh meat, were piled up on the seats and back of the vehicle. One of the men had a machete in his hands and was effectively cutting slices through any walking dead that got too close. I spotted Griffin in the entrance, his sour smile playing on his lips. As we left the last of the promenade behind I saw more dead flowing along the road towards the shops, as the scent of meat and the farmer's men were drawing them in. How long before they were all decomposed and rotten, I wondered? When would it end?

I became more adept at clipping and spinning away the dead that got in our way, rather than messily hitting them square on and letting the wheels chew the life out of them.

'Do you know the way?' Summer said as we left the village.

'I think so,' I said. I'd driven past the wind farm many times on patrol.

68

We found the road that led us to the wind turbines. The giant white structures must have been ninety metres tall and sat on the rolling green hill like Martian machines. I was relieved to see that a high metal fence surrounded them, keeping the compound secure. The fence was topped by razor wire, and I wondered what Jack had in mind for the fences around the village. The man clearly had a problem with me, but if he had the know-how to keep us all safe I would live with it.

We followed the fence line and picked up the dirt track that led to the gates. I could see there was already a white transit van at the entrance. Slowing down, I parked the 4x4 ten metres behind its rear bumper.

'Wait here,' I told them and stepped out. It was an exposed hillside, and I could feel the wind whipping through my clothes and chilling me to the bone. Glancing in every direction, I was relieved there were no bodies following us. Leaving my twelve bore in the vehicle I drew out an extendable. Creeping up to the rear doors of the transit van I tried to look in through the dirty rear windows. It was dark inside the interior and I couldn't make out any movement. Down the side of the vehicle, I could see that the driver's door wasn't closed all the way. I drew the baton back over my shoulder for leverage and wrenched the door open. The cab was empty and the key still hung out of the ignition. Suddenly I felt a pressure on my shoulder and the baton was ripped out of my hand.

'You could have my eye out with that.' It was the rotund electrician Bob Sack, and he had a broad smile on his face.

'What the fuck are you doing?' I said in a breathless whisper.

'Sorry mate, I've always been light on my feet. Do you want a sit down?' Bob said.

Summer and Lester had come over now the danger appeared over. Bob seemed sheepish when he saw the look on Summer's face, and changed the subject.

'I've crowbarred the padlock off and replaced it with one of my own. The last thing we want is any more of those things following us into the compound.'

'Let's get the right side of this fence then,' I said.

We drove our vehicles up the winding gravel driveway. The turbines rose above us and dwarfed us like ants. The unmoving blades hung in space and, as we drew nearer, we saw the unique aerodynamic curve and shape of the smooth white blades. They were a giant engineering feat unlikely to be matched by us few human survivors.

'So these things power the village?' Summer asked as I parked.

'Bob seems to think so.'

Outside again Bob was getting his tools together. Lester found an old cigarette to smoke and appeared content.

'Do you know what you're doing?' I said to Bob, watching him pick up and disregard various tools I was clueless as to the purpose of. Bob gave me a funny smile. I was beginning to think he was a bit strange.

I could see doors on each of the three massive turbine bases.

'So what now then, Bob?'

'The village gets most of its electricity from this wind farm. The high winds up on the fells made it environmentally viable, although of course there were still plenty of objections from local residents.'

'What local residents Bob?' I said smiling and looking around. I couldn't see anything other than rolling, grassy fells. A quarter mile down the track, I could just make out the gate. No bodies had gathered yet.

'So Bob, can you fix it?' Summer asked, smiling.

70

'I won't know until we get into the control room. Come on,' he said.

It was clear that Lester did not want to come out and play. He sat in the back of the 4x4 and had produced another tinny from his pocket. I motioned for him to roll the window down.

'Are you coming with us, Lester?'

'Are you joking, Officer?'

I went into the driver's side and took out the keys.

'You can be a look out Lester. If anyone comes you hit the horn.'

'Best leave those keys then.'

Five previous convictions for vehicle theft.

'Lester,' I said. 'Get real.'

I walked over to the middle turbine base. Bob had already opened the door. The three of us looked at each other for a second. I went first with the twelve bore and Summer followed close behind.

The narrow ladder smelt of dust and oil. Ten feet down, we were in a corridor clustered with wires and pipes. I could see numerous electrical panels and boxes at intervals. The place was spacious, like a Tardis.

'Where to start?' I said.

'I've got a theory,' Bob said. 'Yesterday and last night when all this craziness started up we had storms and high winds up here. Really high. Too high for these turbines even. In fact, I think they are programmed to shut down when the winds pick up too much to prevent the blades and mechanisms becoming damaged. For whatever reason they never started up again.'

Bob pushed ahead of us and around the corner, seemingly oblivious to any danger. We caught him up bent over a board of flashing lights. He started to flick some switches down one side and there was a great whirring in

71

the machinery above. He spent another half hour on the panel as the crescendo of raw noise engulfed us.

'There you go. Easy as pie,' he shouted as Summer and I looked at each other uneasily. It was deafening.

We climbed back up, and outside I ducked instinctively as the giant blades whipped down from the first turbine.

'Two hundred miles per hour and twenty two revolutions a minute. Impressive, hey?' shouted Bob again. He was already on his way into the next turbine base.

I looked back towards Lester and the 4x4.

'Shit,' both Summer and I mouthed at the same time. It wasn't a Lester problem this time. I could see half a dozen walking dead edging their way over the crest of the hill. They weren't coming from the direction of the gate, but from the fence line itself. Lester had seen them too and his face held a more serious expression than usual. Bob hadn't even noticed and had disappeared, I presumed into the next turbine.

'Let's run them down,' Summer screamed to me above the noise.

We jumped into the 4x4 and I revved the engine wildly. I sped forward and nearly stalled as I made a harsh, tearing turn on the gravel.

The first man was stumbling at speed towards us. His jaw bone was unhinged and one foot looked loose and broken as it flopped around with each stride. I clipped him with one corner of the vehicle at fifteen mph. I expected to knock him off his feet, but instead he was launched into the air. His head bulls-eyed off the windscreen and turned the glass into a patchwork of spider webs.

'Reverse over him,' Summer shouted.

I could see in my mirrors that the man was attempting to rise. I crunched into reverse and ploughed the two tonne vehicle over the top of his head. It was pulped into the earth.

'Give me a little room with the next one,' she shouted over.

She leant right out of the passenger window and buried her hatchet in the head of a woman reaching desperately for us. The hatchet lodged in deep, and the woman folded onto her knees and her head collapsed awkwardly into the grass.

'Remind me to get that later,' Summer said, looking crazy and elated.

The next three went down by old fashioned death by dangerous driving. In the old days, you could get fourteen years for the offence, but today all you had to worry about was breaking your vehicle on their decomposing, inhuman carcasses. The 4x4 did the job with ease.

The diesel gauge was down to a quarter of a tank. I planned to siphon fuel out of the unused patrol cars. There were three spare diesel vehicles back at the station.

My mind snapped back to reality when I saw what had breached the fence. In the hollow lay the smouldering remains of an over-turned police car. Behind it the steel fence was torn and twisted. I counted two bodies down on their knees scrabbling for a way through the broken windows. I'd seen enough nature documentaries to recognise animals feeding. I pulled the 4x4 alongside and stopped.

'Are you sure you really want to see this, Johnny?' Summer said.

'That's fucking disgusting,' Lester added from the back.

I got out the vehicle and raised the twelve bore. I fired two shots into the backs and spinal cords of the two feeding men. It might not kill them outright but at least it disabled them and made it safer to be near. Bending down I craned to look inside the wreck. Bracing for an awful sight, I knew enough about these things already to guess one of my colleagues must still have the remnants of life.

'Hello mate,' I said, staring into the ruined face of Rogers, the one police officer who was unaccounted for yesterday. He was suspended upside down by his seat belt. I guess he hadn't stuck with the infected and deceased sergeant Dolan after all, not that it made much difference in the end. On the road behind the fence, I could see a broken zombie. I guessed they had swerved to avoid him, perhaps not knowing that the rules had changed.

'Johnny,' came a hissing reply. It could see blood bubbles on Rogers' lips. It brought back memories of the seal on the beach.

'Are you okay?' I said, ridiculously.

'I don't feel so good. Is there an ambulance coming?'

'Yes, I'm sure they won't be long,' I said. I didn't know what to say to him. 'Shall I get you out?'

'You can't do that mate. I'm broken, I can feel my bones all moving. Those people, they bit me. I thought they were going to help me but they just wouldn't stop eating at me.'

It was dark with shadow in the interior but I could see nearly everything awash with blood. There were mouth-sized gouges all over his face, bare tendon and cheek bone exposed to see. His legs looked crushed by the impacted dashboard. I knew there was nothing I could do.

'You shot them and look they are still moving. I don't understand ... any of this.' Rogers struggled. 'I just feel so tired now.'

I watched him slip into some sort of deep sleep.

'Rogers!' I said loudly.

When he didn't rouse or move I shot him once in the face. It seemed the kindest thing under the circumstances. I wondered if I would ever forget or be able to sleep again. I walked back to the 4x4. Already the two dead I'd shot were trying to crawl away. What remained in the overturned vehicle no longer held any interest to their sick senses.

'Well done,' Summer managed. In the back, Lester was making loud gulps on his tinny.

Back at the turbines, Bob appeared finished and was waiting patiently in his white transit van. Two of the three turbine blades rotated at speed.

'I got them going,' said Bob. 'But they won't last us forever. Cyclic stresses will destroy them in the end, and there ain't nothing I can do about that. But we could have a few years of power here.'

'Okay, Bob,' I said. 'Let's go back to the village.'

CHAPTER 12

The green Land Rover was followed by a motley stream of vehicles down the lane to Jack's farm. Griffin and his father's show of strength back at the WI had persuaded over half the people present that their best chance in the crazy new world was to leave behind the isolation of their own dwellings and join the promised stronghold at Jack's place. He had sold them the idea that the high tensile fence was the only way to keep this enemy at bay, and talked of a collective, of everyone working together in a new community at the farm. They wanted – *they needed* – to be part of this. People wanted to survive.

The vehicles began to park in what space they could find around the muddied yard. Griffin Nation was already out and prowling around with a loaded gun in his hands.

Toby and Jean Hanson frowned at each other with worried expressions, both wondering if this foul smelling, run down old farmhouse was really where they wanted to be.

'What a shit hole,' Phillip, their twelve year old son said loudly.

Jack Nation was standing close enough to hear. 'Great kid you have there.'

'Are those more dead people there?' their other child Mark said, pointing.

The adults all looked across the yard and saw the five human forms semi-submerged in cow muck near the barn.

'Don't worry, we'll get those cleared up in no time,' Jack said.

'More hands make tidy work,' Griffin added and gave his best gap-toothed smile.

A woman wearing a red coat emerged from the farmhouse front door.

'Have you been alright, Alison?' Jack called. He woman had a slightly skittish and haunted look about her, and didn't seem to want to reply.

'Is our Dexter still unwell?' Jack pressed on.

'No change,' she said not meeting his eyes. She saw Jean Hanson then and smiled. 'When's it due?'

'Two months give or take,' she replied. 'I don't know how we'll cope now.'

Jean was starting to cry. Alison and a few other women who had heard came forward as if to comfort her.

'Let's go inside and get some tea,' Alison suggested.

'Yes, that would be good,' Jean said. 'Boys, you are coming in too.'

The men were left outside staring at Jack and Griffin.

'Right, lets get this shit hole cleared up shall we,' Jack said, eyeing Toby. 'And then we can make some plans.'

By the evening, the new arrivals had been assigned new rooms in the farmhouse; attics, storerooms and parlours filled up with people. The shortage of beds meant that most people had to make do with blankets and cushions on the hard wooden boards. Jack and Griffin made it clear from the start that this would be temporary, and they'd build some more permanent accommodation next door. 'Turn the barn into a fortress. Planners don't have no say no more, we can do what we fucking please,' Jack had said.

The farmhouse kitchen was abuzz with activity as a tropical haze of steam evaporated from the numerous pots and pans bubbling and hissing on the hobs. Alison had led a few of the other woman in preparing a stew, which according to Jack was the best way to feed so many new mouths. As she stirred the boiling vegetables and meat, she had never had felt so unsettled in her life. Her husband had turned into some kind of monster, had tried to kill her. Her life had been saved by Griffin and Jack, farmers, a world

77

away from the life she had at the bank in the city. It seemed Jack would keep her safe, but as always, there was a price to be paid. What he had done last night when he came into her room made her feel numb inside, but to survive she had to live with it.

'We need more chairs,' Jack told Griffin as he made arrangements around the large kitchen table. 'People will have to eat in stages.'

'Right then,' said Griffin and called over some of the other men. 'There's more out in one of the garages.'

The men returned as huge steaming bowls of broth were placed on the table. Everyone began to file in and take their seats, with Jack making sure he had the head of the table all to himself. He patted the seat next to him and obediently Alison came over and sat down. She gave a forced smile and looked at the sea of new faces. They looked worried and stressed, maybe a little like concentration camp survivors she wondered.

'No one stands on ceremony around here. Come on tuck in everyone,' Jack said.

'Shouldn't we say grace,' a small, spectacled man at the end of the table said weakly.

'If you think it would help go ahead. Myself, I think God has left the building,' Jack said and Griffin led a few chuckles.

'Lord may we be thankful for what we are about to receive ...' the spectacled man went on. Alison tuned out and looked across at Jack. She could tell he was mad because the ruddy lines of capillaries on his cheek flushed with red. Jack was a man with a temper, she knew that already.

'Thank you for that,' Jack said harshly as knives and forks began to clink and scrape on the china. 'As I said back at the Institute, I've got an idea that I think can save us all.'

'Build a bloody big fence,' chipped in Griffin.

'I've got stacks of high tensile fencing stored up in the barn which I never got chance to put to good use. It's not enough of course but it's a start. We can get more of the stuff from other farms I know around here that have as much stock as I do,' Jack continued. 'It'll be hard work, not pen pushing in some bloody office. Your soft hands won't know what's hit 'em. We'll sink the fence posts deep and concrete them in. Set them wide because we have a lot of country to cover. Then we'll lay a line of the toughest fence you ever saw and all those dead things will be able to do is stand there and whistle, cause they won't be visiting no more.'

'Sounds brilliant,' Toby Hanson said. Others around the table agreed. Alison was already warming to the Hansons. She wanted their baby to be safe.

'I'll pray tonight that it works,' the spectacled man added.

'You do that,' Griffin snarled.

Later the plates were cleared and the dark evening drew on into night. Pockets of people grouped around the farmhouse rooms and tried to establish a little private space. Jack had handed out candles after he decided the low, flickering light would act as less of a beacon. People stood at the windows and stared out over the dark fields, fearful of what might be wandering amongst rutted furrows. It was too dark for anyone to be sure they were alone, but as the hours ticked by no more bodies came stumbling into the farmyard. Eventually people grew weary and drifted off to their makeshift sleeping quarters. Everyone knew now that dangerous days of work lay ahead.

Alison went up to the room she now shared with Jack. It was horribly old-fashioned, like a relic from the 1970's. Pictures of Jack's wife seemed to cover all the walls and the dressing table. In the candle light, she felt there were a thousand ghostly eyes on her, the dead wife watching her every move. The stair boards down the hallway creaked, already Jack's heavy boot steps were unmistakeable to her. It made her stomach sink and swim with butterflies. She didn't know if it was fear or excitement.

The door opened and there he was. 'A good day,' he called it. He removed his tweedy farmer's clothes that smelled richly of soil and animal waste. His body appeared strong in some muscle groups, but his chest was sagging as age and gravity took their toll. In places, his skin looked tired and wrinkled, the elasticity used up.

Alison withdrew back across the bed to make sure he had plenty of space. She didn't want him to touch her but knew inevitably that he would. The candles went out one by one and then he was next to her, breathing his rasping breaths into her ear.

'I'd like it if I could call you Millie in bed. Would you do that for me?'

She told him 'yes,' he could use his dead wife's name. She knew she loathed him then. But what could she do? Outside on her own she would die quickly, perhaps turn into one of those monsters.

Pyjamas pulled free, his bulk started to press down on her and between her legs. Jack grunted down like a beast, like a wild hog at feeding time. His noise must have woken Dexter because he began to howl and moan in the next room along.

'He has to go out,' he said, stopping. Alison felt too frightened to reply. She knew what Dexter had become.

Alison felt Jack move off her and saw his bulky outline start to re-dress in the darkness. She could hear other people start to stir in the farmhouse as Dexter's loud howls continued.

'His gag must have worked its way loose,' Jack said matter-of-factly. 'I can't be dealing with him in the house any longer.'

Alison could picture Dexter strapped to his bed, bailing wires cutting into the greying skin of his wrists and ankles. The crude rags thrust deep down his throat by Jack had dislodged. It hardly mattered because whatever thing Dexter had transformed into no longer seemed to crave oxygen as part of its existence. He would lay dormant for prolonged periods and then seemed to explode with fearsome rages, eyes protruding out of their sockets like chunks of jet stone. She knew Jack had kept the door locked and off-limits, telling none of the new arrivals why.

Alison stayed in bed as he heard Jack leave the bedroom and talk in hushed, mumbled tones with Griffin in the corridor. Bangs and crashes followed in the minutes afterwards as they bundled Dexter out of his room. She heard the heavy bang of the front door over the lash of wind and rain hitting the window.

Alison looked down as Jack and Griffin carried the thrashing body of Dexter towards the barn. She could see the farmyard had become a brown pit of flowing mud as they slipped and struggled. The three passed out of her line of sight as an explosion cracked in the air. A blinding flash of light followed and illuminated the fields and woods. She thought she saw the silhouette of more dark figures up at the tower.

A storm was upon us.

CHAPTER 13

The trainer shoe twitched in the seawater pool, flicking up a fine spray. The foot inside the trainer shifted again and the body slowly picked itself upright once again. In the week since it had transformed, the man had stumbled and fallen hundreds of times when roaming around the rocky beaches and peninsulas that led from Haven around the horseshoe bay. Initial grazing of grey skin in these falls had given way to raw, bloodless wounds and open fractures around both knees.

Alan Temple no longer remembered setting off from his bungalow in the heart of the village to set off on his regular five mile run along the beach and woodland trails. Neither did he remember leaving his wife of more than ten years behind with a kiss and a promise of a night of fine dining. Alan did not recall laughter in his four year old daughter's face when he tickled her ribs and left.

As Alan's feet dragged strange, ragged grooves through the wet sand past the bloating carcass of a dead seal he didn't really think much of anything anymore. He no longer consciously knew his way anywhere; he had become a creature of pure instincts. At some point a blinding pain had placed his mind in a vice and squeezed it shut. What followed was like a black cancer; an invisible, chemical force that stripped out his identity and dissolved it into a metaphorical acid bath.

Alan no longer had the memories or the daydreams that used to flow so willingly. The kernel that remained was an intangible, heartless need to feed on the living. Nothing mattered in his world anymore other than the sweet caress of hot blood and organs, and the overwhelming, nihilistic, primitive desire to wipe the flesh off every living thing. Alan steered an arbitrary course away from the seal and staggered inland. His stuttering steps picked their way off the beach and finally found a shallow incline onto the woodland path. He moved slowly but, like a shark, never stopped.

The sounds of living creatures chattering and scratching around in the woods led him quickly off the path and into a steep climb through thick, brambled foliage. Alan moved forward, oblivious to the ripe thorns tearing dark lines across his face. His senses had changed and mutated. No longer dominated by sight, he followed a jumbled blur of all six. He sensed the vibrations of living things on the stilled air and moved to follow. Small, wild rabbits danced mockingly around his feet as he swept his hands around in windmill motions and fell over again. His dirty fingers reached into the earth and smeared wood lice into his mouth. They hung oozing and half-alive from his lips; a grotesque spectacle.

Pushing his way over a crumbling dry stone wall he found himself in a huge field with a steep downward slope. A few small trees and scatterings of scree marked out the barren grassy space. Alan should have remembered bringing his daughter Jennifer up there in the winter snow, and her giggling screams of 'again, again' after every race of the plastic sledges. He remembered nothing and no longer noticed the picture postcard views of the village and the watery sweep of the bay beyond.

Gravity took hold of his legs and sped him down the field that, under different circumstances, may have even appeared comical. He tumbled again over a barbed wire fence that raked an ugly tear through his tattered Nike t-shirt into the muscle of his abdomen. Like a clockwork machine, he picked himself up again and walked on. No attention to the other human figures in the field, his senses tuned to the fact that they were also walking dead, as aimless and directionless as he. Gravity took his hand again and led him down the tarmac road into the village, past houses cold and empty inside.

Further and he felt something drawing him closer. He passed broken and ruined cars, one with the bloodied face of a woman clawing at the windows to find release. Noticing her, in a flickering instant he discarded her as non-living and unwanted. A row of detached houses stretched before him and made him pause and flick his head back and forth like a lizard. Something buried fathoms deep told him he had been here before, in a life out of reach but not all forgotten. Alan passed one door and then another, finally stopping dead centre at one coloured sickest green. A grey hand reached out and pressed against the door, and by pure chance caught on the handle and flicked it down. The lever sprang and the PVC door opened inward.

The small toy was held tightly in a clammy grip. The origin of the blue animal was unclear, with its hide plucked clean of fur and its ears torn and misshapen. Little fingers gripped and plucked at the toy, doing as any adult would with a stress reliever. The owner of the small hands had a pretty face, an angel's face her Mummy had told her. She loved it when her Mummy combed her hair and tied it back in beautiful bows, hair that now hung in restless knots over her face. Her Mummy wasn't well but she would be back soon, she often thought, just like my Daddy will.

She was scared all the time but especially when it got dark. She was scared of the things outside, the people who were not well like Mummy. She used to stand at the window and wave, but then they banged and banged to come inside and she hadn't dared go back to the window again. She was getting hungry now and the fridge smelled bad. She had tried, but couldn't open tins like Mummy and Daddy could. When it went dark, she felt safer in the cupboard under the stairs. It was always her favourite place to hide when she played hide and seek. It was her best game.

There were noises in the house now, footsteps creaking down the hallway towards her. Shifting in the dark, she looked through the crack in the door to try and see who was there. A flash of a pair of dirty shoes and running tights she had seen before. She knew them because they were what her Daddy always wore.

'I missed you so much,' she shouted out, running from her hiding place.

The thing that had once been her father called Alan looked down. It bent low to give her an awful kiss.

'Daddy that hurts ... Daddy stop please ... Da ...'

CHAPTER 14

Bob Sack sat in the flat bed lorry taken from a nearby haulage firm and reversed it up to the fence line. On the ground, Jack had found a white hard hat and stood bellowing orders like any building site foreman. The villagers scurried around like dutiful worker ants and began off-loading the heavy wooden posts from the lorry, along with yet another vast roll of wire.

Griffin operated the shovel excavator from the back of the farm's tractor, boring deep holes into the hard, frozen earth. Stretching over one quarter of a mile across the fields stood their engineering endeavour; a seven foot high fence sunk into concrete, strung with gleaming, spaghetti-thick, taut silver wire. Jack told them it would hold back an army of the dead.

They had slaved through field after field for the best part of a week now, losing an average of a person a day to attacks from the bodies. Mainly it had been in the beginning, when Jack had worked them into the twilight hours. The dead's shuffling approach had been missed in the fatigue and shadows. They were better prepared now.

'Can you see any movement out there?' Toby Hanson said to his wife. They were taking a turn on sentry duty and had a panoramic view of the rolling fields from the top of an unhitched farm trailer. Toby held a broken barrelled shotgun over the crook of his arm.

Jean Hanson didn't answer, and instead stared almost constantly back towards the farmhouse, as she had done for much of the day. Mark and Phillip were inside with the other children, safe and warm with Alison and some of the older, less able people.

'You know nobody would mind if you went back there. Everyone can see how pregnant you are.'

'Jack would mind, you know that. We all have to pull our weight,' she said in hushed tones.

Already they were both wary of the man who was leading them. They had watched him have a hand in the death of every new bitten person in the past week; his face always the same expressionless mask to their final pleas. The world they lived in had become a brutal, ugly place.

Griffin strode past and ignored them.

'I'm going to check on the farm and a few other things,' he said, with a nod to Jack to take over on the excavator.

Griffin jumped on his quad bike and motored down the fields. He thought progress had been slow but he still hoped the whole village would be safe behind the fence by the end of winter. *Until then there is still fun to be had.*

Back in the farmyard, he spent the briefest of time exchanging pleasantries with his father's new girlfriend, Alison. He liked to glance at her big milk breasts when she wasn't looking. They were so big they could be plumped up pillows filling out his mother's old patchwork wool jumpers. Alison was getting on a bit, but he still wanted to touch them one day if his father let him.

'Are you sure you don't want a cup of tea, Griffin?'

He looked around at the noisy, annoying kids getting underfoot and the old people cluttering up his house.

'No, I'm going out to the barn to check on Dexter.'

Jack had insisted on keeping Dexter alive, but thankfully now out of the house. Why he wanted to keep Dexter around at all was a mystery to him. He respected his father more than anyone and would loyally follow him into anything. But it was clear to Griffin that what now inhabited the barn had nothing in common with his brother, other than a crumbling outward appearance. It scared him but at the same time opened up dizzying feelings of morbid curiosity. Griffin loved too that the barn remained something of a mystery among the new comers. He often caught snatches of the conspiring whispers, but whatever they thought or said it didn't change the fact that the barn was totally off limits; it was his and his father's secret alone.

He knew they needed him and Jack to stay alive. The power had shifted and these people couldn't look down their noses anymore from fancy houses and flash new cars. *Without me and Dad you'd all be ripped to pieces*, he smiled.

Griffin went to the barn door and wrestled a key into the heavy padlock. The tattered wooden door shuddered open with a hard pull, creaking on hinges out of alignment and caked in rust.

It smelled bad inside, not just of animals long departed but a new smell of rotting human flesh. Sparkling beams of light flowed through holes in the broken roof, partially illuminating a large, green tarpaulin that hung over one of the animal pens like a crude tent. Griffin's hands sweated as he pulled one flap up and looked into the crazed eyes of his shackled brother.

He didn't seem to need food, or sleep, or much of anything human anymore.

'I know what you want Dexter. You want a piece of this fresh meat, don't you?' Griffin said, carefully staying out of reach of his grasping, groaning brother. Griffin turned and bared his buttocks.

'Well sorry brother, rump is off the menu today.'

Griffin pulled the tarpaulin back into place, standing still a moment or two to let his brother calm down. He wasn't the real reason why he was in the barn. In the pen next door to Dexter there was a figure lying on the dirty straw floor. She had a woman's shapely curves but the same granite pallor as his brother. Griffin had her bound horizontally with her arms stretched taut like a crucifixion. Ropes held her waist anchored flat and an old tennis ball protruded awkwardly from her mouth, making it impossible for her to bite. She was a killing machine made all but helpless, and best of all, she was all his.

Griffin didn't recognise her as somebody from the village and had found her wandering near the tower on a misty morning two days earlier. If asked he wouldn't be able to say precisely why he had taken her and hidden her away. A harmless piece of fun, he'd told his father.

Griffin looked down at those curves again and slipped the scaling knife out of his back pocket. Button by button he cut open her silken blouse and then started on her bra. She was beautiful like a grey statue from a museum. Thrashing hard at her binds, he knew that she wanted him. He loved her ripe blackberry nipples, flicking them with the edge of his blade. Was it time to cut them off?

'Not yet my dear,' he whispered, beginning to loosen his belt.

CHAPTER 15

Summer and I were looking out of an upstairs window of the police station, watching the zombies pass by. Lester had woken us early in an excited mood. In the four weeks since the outbreak, he'd managed to kick the booze habit and his human hygiene had improved markedly. He'd also evidently purloined Rogerson's civvies out of the locker room, and had discarded the onion skin tramp clothing.

Without the alcohol in his system, he actually started to have civilised conversations, and Summer and I had learned that in his past life he had been a science teacher. We'd not yet asked what event in his life had driven him to drink and the streets, but we guessed it wouldn't be pretty.

'So Lester, why exactly have you woken us up so early?' Summer said.

'You're a pretty girl, Summer,' he answered. 'But your memory is like a goldfish. I told you already, today we're going to find out what makes these dead things tick.'

I shook my head and wandered off to get a coffee.

In the end, we cleaned the evidence of Lester's carnage and made the police station our home. I don't precisely know why we did this, but I guessed it was mainly because it was the part of the village we knew best and the station was where we felt safest.

Surprisingly only a few of the locals had come to join us in the station. Nearly everyone else still drawing breath had either moved to the farm or left the village completely. Bill Thomas and his boyfriend Arthur had been waiting outside when we returned from the wind farm. Bill was small, and looked uncannily like Michael J Fox, while Arthur was more rotund, and quite hidden behind an unruly salt and pepper beard.

Later, they talked to us over beers. Arthur told me how Bill thought I looked sexy in the Women's Institute meeting and how they thought farmers smelled of cow poo and had no class. They also said their basement flat on the Haven promenade had become overrun by the walking dead and they'd never go back.

We had picked up Jefferson a week later on one of our food runs to Tomlinson's. He'd actually been the one to finish off the old crone of an owner, who we had locked in her store cupboard and left to twirl and crash. Jefferson was a sixty-five year old widower but was still young at heart. Stick thin, and gaunt faced, Jefferson was our man of mystery. He kept to himself, and could play a mean game of chess. While Bill and Arthur slept happily in each other's arms in one of the offices, Jefferson welcomed me into the refreshment room with a wave of his cup of tea. The old guy was a terrible insomniac.

'How are you doing, Jeff?'

'Not too bad, son. I hope that nut box Lester hasn't got you into one of his schemes. What does that crazy bastard have in mind this time?'

'Don't ask Jefferson, just don't ask. The really crazy thing is that he halfway knows what he is doing. I'm just going to go with the flow, I've decided.'

Jefferson grunted amusement and we sipped hot drinks, conversation drying up.

'Think I might just go for a walk,' Jefferson said.

'So Lester isn't the only crazy one,' I replied. But in truth I knew Jefferson was a tough old bird who could take care of himself, and no outbreak of the dead people was going to stop him doing exactly what he wanted to do.

'Have you finished gassing yet?' Lester said, popping his head around the door. 'Me and Summer are more than ready to do this thing.'

This thing involved a long rope, a baseball bat and a pair of rigid handcuffs according to Lester. It was a truly mad plan, but in the weeks since Lester had sobered up, he had worn us down on the idea.

'I've been watching this small one for a while now, it's been hanging out in the back car park for a few days. It's in just the right condition for what we want.'

'Okay, whatever you say, Lester,' Summer said, and smiled at me.

We all took some deep breaths and went outside. I felt the cold prickle at my skin and knew the winter months were definitely near. I hoped those wind turbines would hold up. Mine and Summer's breath plumed as we waited for the signal from Lester. He walked forward and caught the attention of the body. The postman was short and had been around forty years of age when he died. In the last four weeks his clothes had become shredded and caked in so many layers of dirt that the original blues were no longer distinguishable.

'I think his name's Trevor,' I said to Summer through my riot gear helmet. Due to the decay and rot in the man's face it was hard to be sure.

'Alright, Trevor,' Summer smiled.

Lester was in human bait mode. Trevor started to gather momentum the far end of the car park, and Summer and I fanned out wide looking out for any other bodies coming in off the main road. Thankfully, early morning seemed to be their most docile time.

The man's elongated lope gathered more speed and Lester waved him on. Ten metres out and Summer and I closed in a pincer movement. We each picked up one end of the rope and yanked, as the body tripped and fell in an ugly heap.

Summer picked up the bat and with real relish clonked Trevor square on the ass as he was trying to rise.

He gave out a low moan and spreadeagled again, as Lester shouted 'DON'T HIT THE HEAD' for around the fifth time.

It was my turn next as I descended on to the flattened body and kneeled on its back. Wearing my thickest leather gloves, I wrestled my handcuffs onto the man's wrists in a messy hybrid formation.

'My God, it worked Lester,' I said stepping away. 'Now let's get this fucker inside.'

'TO THE LAB!' pointed Lester.

'Stop shouting, you two,' Summer said. Numerous bodies were entering the car park.

'Come on,' I hissed.

Lester and I took an elbow each and dragged the body towards the back door. Its arm skin felt loose and mushy, and the smell was rancid meat. Trevor snapped his teeth at each one of us in turn, unsure which one of us he wanted to rip to pieces first. We didn't give him the chance and wrenched our way to the door.

Already, three walking dead inhabited the space where we'd cuffed the dead man, and quicker than Trevor, were now hurtling towards us.

'Inside,' I shouted, as Summer punched the key code and flung the door open.

We stumbled over the threshold and back into the drying room. Almost immediately, the other bodies started thumping on the door to join us, so we dragged Trevor away into the report writing room. Summer moved ahead and opened more doors as we frogmarched our guest all the way through the police station to the cell block.

Summer flicked the lights on and we went into the cell Lester had prepared earlier. In the centre was a freshly assembled Ikea kitchen table Lester had ratted out of some unfortunate's garage a week earlier. On the table were four heavy leather straps bolted into the wood, and several extra straps ready for Trevor's head.

'Welcome to the slab, motherfucker,' I said, forcing Trevor the last few feet.

After much struggling and just a few bruises, we got the thrashing body tightly strapped down on the table.

'I made juice,' Summer said bringing in a jug of orange squash. We needed a break.

'So what's the plan now, Professor Lester?' I asked.

'Now we do some sawing and maybe chopping too,' he said, rummaging through the impressive array of tools he had lain out on the floor. The centrepiece was a tatty looking bone saw that Lester had found in the house of the deceased local GP, Dr. Phillips.

'Is this going to get messy?' Summer asked and Lester just smiled. We were impressed with him. In the past few weeks, he'd really pulled himself together. He looked almost scholarly in his doctor's apron and scrubs.

'Well, I'm not clearing it up,' she said with a shrug. 'Trevor is going to get messy.'

'So, we're pretty sure that these things are textbook zombies, right?' I interrupted. 'The re-animated undead that want to eat you. Shoot 'em in the head and it's lights out and goodnight.'

'Johnny's right, Trevor be straight out of a movie,' added Summer, looking down that the drooling, groaning thing we had on the table. We had become used to the smell to some extent. Four weeks surrounded by walking, rotting bodies does that for you. But because the cell we were inside was relatively small we all had Vicks ointment smeared liberally under our noses.

'Right, children,' Lester said, waving a bread knife in the air. 'It's down to business time.'

'How does he know where to start cutting?' Summer whispered to me, as we both winced at the gory scene unfolding in front of us.

'I heard that. Trust me I'm a scientist.'

Lester started by tearing off the man's dirty t-shirt. Underneath he had a surprisingly hairy chest on pallid grey skin.

'Sean Connery, eat your heart out!' I said to Summer, who looked blank.

'What?'

Lester drew some lines on Trevor's chest in permanent marker and then started revving up the wood saw. The man on the table seemed momentarily distracted by the din, before going back to baring his bloody-black teeth at us. Lester started sawing in a vertical line over the man's sternum. Congealed, clotted blood spat out in every direction, painting the walls, ceiling, and us. The man's chest flesh tore open like a rotten peach and Lester reached down and ripped the putrefied pulped fat off in liberal chucks, throwing them into a plastic bucket next to his feet with a dull *splat*. The man's eyes bulged, but Trevor didn't seem to being feeling much pain. That was perhaps just as well.

'Bone time,' Lester said swiping blood off his ski goggles.

The saw went into the ribcage with the high pitch of a dentist's drill gone wild. Lester made a trap door shape in the man's chest and then wrenched it away with a terrible *crunch*. We all stared down at the man's organs with interest. They looked vaguely normal, if very gammed up with clotted blood.

'Can you see anything moving? 'Cos I can't,' I said, trying to sound calm.

Lester prodded at the man's heart with a pencil. 'Fucker should be dead,' he said. Trevor's gnashing teeth begged to differ.

'Right, brain next,' Lester said.

'This is some messy shit, Lester,' I said. 'I thought you were a scientist.'

'Johnny, I was one of the finest teachers of biology the Queen Elizabeth ever saw. The brain is where it's at. Have we the fish bowl on standby?'

I tapped the bowl with my foot and the white vinegar swished around. 'Proceed.'

'Now this won't hurt a bit, Trevor,' Lester soothed, and re-started the wood saw. He brought it down on an area of cranium just above his left ear, and buzzed his way as Summer and I ducked the bone shrapnel coming our way.

'Well, I may have gone a little too deep,' Lester shouted over the din. Trevor's eyes crazy bulges.

'We got his attention now, alright,' Summer shouted.

The skull cap flopped to cell room floor with just a little tugging, and Lester swapped the bone saw for an every day kitchen ladle. 'We ready to pop this baby?'

I looked down at Trevor's pulsating black brain, like a cauliflower lost in a bath of treacle.

'Err ...'

'Now watch,' Lester said, and delved straight into Trevor's head with the ladle. 'One good turn deserves another,' he added, trying to twist it free.

Just then, Bill and Arthur appeared at the door.

'Anything we can do to ...' Arthur managed, before he was hurling chunks down his beard.

'Don't be a pussy, Arthur,' Bill shouted at his partner. 'It's only a little zombie brain.'

'Do you think we should have told them?' I whispered to Summer.

'One thing's is a definite, Johnny. I'm not clearing this room up, ever. Gross!'

Lester kept wiggling the ladle inside Trevor's head, and finally the brain was out with a *plop* and a *splash*. Trevor snuffed out like a candle.

CHAPTER 16

We passed a message to those working on the endless fence that we wanted another meeting at the Woman's Institute. The workers had a thin, haunted look now like pictures on the police station walls of 1890's poor house prisoners. Jack had them working from dawn into the night nearly every day. We would see the glow of the generator spot lights from the police station and every hour hear shots ring out as another body got too close.

The fence line was an impressive endeavour I had to admit. It stretched nearly a mile from the coast, past Jack's farm and into the fringes of the village itself. Another few months and the fence would be all the way back to the coast again, and the village would, in theory, be zombie free.

For my own reasons I'd kept myself and the others that had stayed at the police station separate from the collective at the farm. Summer, Lester, Bill, Arthur and even Jefferson all kept busy on other tasks, mainly killing bodies and burning them in grand funeral pyres. We systematically went house to house, clearing out the dead and undead, and collecting useful items such as tinned food and fuel to store back at the station or hand out to the workers.

Each one of us became experts at moving through a house room by room, listening for tell-tale sounds of the dead and being ready with our own brand of ultra violence. Jokingly, we called ourselves the SKUL team: Special Killers of Undead Life.

Each had their weapons of choice. With Summer, it was always a hatchet or axe. Bill and Arthur had short, razor-sharp daggers that went through zombie heads like a hot knife through butter. Lester had cleaned and oiled up a WWII German Luger pistol he'd dug out of some Nazi war criminal's loft. Always trust Lester to go that extra mile.

Myself, I'd made a sawn off shotgun, like a regular Jessie James bank robber. Jefferson, well, that crazy old man preferred to use his gloved hands. We wore lots of police riot gear and helmets, and made extra protection for vulnerable areas like the neck. We looked like patchwork American footballers.

Today wasn't about killing zombies. We'd called a meeting so Lester could discuss his findings. We went to the WI early and opened the place up to air. It was clear nobody had been inside since the last meeting over five weeks earlier. The chairs were all still set out as they were and polystyrene cups littered the floor. On the stage, Lester busied himself setting up his presentation diagrams and slide show.

'Do you think they'll come?' Summer said to me as we picked up the litter.

I shrugged, but soon enough there was the tell-tale grumble of diesel engines outside and Jack and Griffin were walking in like they owned the place.

'We got your message Johnny ... so where's the fire,' Jack said.

'No fire Jack. We found a few things about the bodies and we thought it would be useful for us all to know ... for all our benefits.'

'Our group is all ears,' said Griffin.

'Your group, Griffin? I thought we were all part of the same happy community,' I replied. 'Now be a good boy. Sit down and pin back your ears.'

'You don't speak to me like that.'

'Listen, Griffin, no offence to your vast intellect and all, but I think what Lester has to say up there on that stage might just save your life one day.'

'Leave the good policeman alone,' Jack hissed, and placed a hand onto Griffin's shoulder. I could see issues down the line.

I turned to Summer and shrugged, and we went and took our seats at the front. A few other villagers had filed in, their hands and faces dirty. Tired faces; every one of them. I wondered how many of them really liked their new farm community. Was it worth putting up with all Jack's shit? I felt very glad I wasn't part of it.

'Ladies ... gentlemen,' Lester began on the stage. 'Thank you for coming all this way again in such difficult circumstances.' He pulled back a cloth sheet on the table and revealed what was left of Trevor's brain bobbing in the fish tank.

'What the fuck is that in aid of?' Griffin shouted out.

'Shut the fuck up and let him tell you,' was my reply.

Lester ploughed on. 'I appreciate this isn't necessarily what you expect from the average Women's Institute meeting, but please bear with me.'

Lester went over and fired up an old slide projector. A large rectangle of white light flickered into life on the wall at the back of the stage.

'This is a slide I made from the blood of the unfortunate Trevor the postman,' Lester continued, and slotted his first slide into place.

The rectangle of light turned into a red globular mess, which Lester then focused until a cluster of clear, jagged bubbles appeared which I knew must be red blood cells. Lester had spent days getting these slides ready. I figured it must have been the most constructive work he'd done after years of drinking himself into oblivion. I was proud of the guy.

'These are dead, clotted cells you can see, and in any normal, not undead person they would not be in this broken and twisted state. It shows me that these things do not transport oxygen around their bodies. I would surmise they would not even need it. I dug through every inch of this unfortunate's body and organs, and it remains to me a

100

complete mystery how they can continue to function when in all reality they should be pushing up daisies.'

'You dragged us all this way to state the bleeding obvious. I thought you were going to tell us something useful today,' Jack said.

'But I've not finished, my farming friend,' Lester said and clicked onto the next slide. It was a picture of a dead domestic cat.

'Apologies again. Due to a distinct lack of rats and mice at my disposal, I had to utilise an unfortunate house cat. As you can see, it is quite dead now. What I can say theoretically is that the saliva that we know can re-animate humans is in fact quite toxic to everything else. Our dear departed tabby here did not come back looking for an all-you-can-eat fish breakfast, but instead died rather peacefully after being nibbled by a body. I'd suggest that at this time the only zombies we have to worry about are ones of the human variety.'

'Are you taking this in Jack? It means the livestock will need better protection or we'll all end up living off food cans from now until forever,' I said.

'Finally, the most interesting thing of all,' Lester continued.

'What's that? Shoot 'em in the brain and they die. Big surprise there!'

'No, Griffin,' Lester continued. 'There are possibly ten year old children in the Amazon who know that's how you kill a zombie. No, that's not what I was about to say,' Lester said and unbuttoned his shirt. 'A little time before I met my good friends Johnny and Summer here, I was bitten. I was bitten right through my clothes and into my skin.'

Lester showed off the ugly, but now healing scar on his shoulder. 'Now I have no doubt that the zombie bastard Sergeant Dolan's saliva flooded that wound, and yet here I still stand living and breathing, and passing on my wisdom. My final hypothesis to you is that there are some people among us who are quite immune to zombie attentions. Not all animals were born equal it would appear.'

'Doesn't help a lot when there's a pack of those things tearing you apart,' Jack said gruffly, and he and Griffin stood up.

'What about a cure Lester,' Summer said. 'Can you make us all immune?'

'I'm sorry, Summer, I was just a biology teacher. I can only hope there are still some real scientists left out there who can do something special. Until then, we just have to make the best of things and be careful.'

'So, how can we find out who else is immune, Lester?' I asked.

'I'll think of something, some test. Just leave it with me.'

'Well, you could stick your hand in a zom's mouth, Johnny, and see how it takes you,' Griffin said, trying to stare me out.

'Go and fuck your cousin or something. Perhaps the mutant gene pool will throw up some more medical miracles for us.'

Griffin charged at me. I sidestepped and clipped him on the side of his head with a short right-handed punch. Griffin's equilibrium scrambled and he skidded to his knees and then rolled onto his back. He started sucking up air like an old Hoover and his eyes looked a little short on focus. I turned quickly towards Jack, anticipating that he'd make a move, or possibly just shoot me.

'Got your number clocked now officer, don't you worry about that,' he said, just standing, looking at me. He helped his rhino of a son to his feet and they walked out the door. The rest of the villagers filed out behind silently. They looked bowed and defeated.

'Didn't quite go to plan, did it?' Summer said, hugging herself close.

'Nope,' I said. 'Lester, hurry up and pack your shit. We need to get back to the station before those fuckers come back.'

I eyed the door, felt relief when I heard the diesel engines start up and drive away.

She looked down at his chest, the sweat glinting cyan shades of blue in the light filtering in from the street. She felt tall up here, like she was rising above it all and she could forget it all. The breath in her chest moved in rasps, and she imagined the icy air dousing the flames of her burning core. Their breath plumed out in clouds of mist and the office windows turned white opaque. Forms and figures shifted beyond the glass, their faces blurred and indistinct. She gasped and outside moans and cries followed as if calling to her. She concentrated her mind and blocked it all out. He touched her bare, chilled shoulders and she felt his wedding ring bite a little on her flesh.

'Johnny ... Johnny ... I love you,' Summer hummed.

Outside the figures paced closer. They wanted to love Johnny too.

CHAPTER 17

Black plastic rubbish bags filled the alleyway. Many were torn and had spilled their putrid contents like a sea of rotting, decaying mulch. Here and there an arm or foot was distinguishable, an indication that humans were now every bit as disposable as the old newspapers that blew around the streets of the city like tumbleweed.

A noise cut through the air, a low whine that became a metallic roar of force. The half dozen ambling bodies on the street craned their maggoty necks in the direction of the vibrations. They sensed it now ... *sustenance*. The bags exploded into their ruined faces, and hulking metal crashed through the end of the alleyway and into the open street. Sickly smells of burnt rubber rose off the dirty asphalt and mingled with the rot. The bodies watched motionless as the metal shape disappeared around a corner and the vibrations receded far into the distance. A part of them still sensed it out there and in unison, they moved to follow.

'Trust the apocalypse to come on a bin day,' Howard said and looked around at the three others in the old VW campervan. Jinny wasn't smiling, and was still ineffectually dabbing at the wound torn through the Jonah's camouflage trousers. The back of the van had become a chaotic jumble of clothing, food and pools of black clotted blood. Barely habitable.

'How's he doing?' shouted Tehgan over the tinny tappets of the engine. She dropped the A-Z map down to her lap and looked back over the front passenger seat.

'He's doing just fine, aren't you Jonah,' Jinny said back to her sister. She wasn't fooling anybody.

They'd been hiding out for over two months in the city, scurrying around like rats, trying to eke out an existence in a crumbling nightclub that had once been a church.

Howard had been a student, drinking until the sun came up. He'd staggered out dazed into the morning sunlight with a handful of student friends, and a shared goal of getting a Macdonald's all-day breakfast. At first he had thought he was witnessing a traffic accident, and inexplicably there were more and more. Metal piling on metal, people running and screaming one way and then another.

It was as if his friends had been washed away in the craziness of it all. All of a sudden, he had been alone on the step of an old church watching a world gone mad. Almost without conscious thought, his feet had taken him back inside and his hands had moved and locked the heavy door behind him. He was glad that he had been drunk when it started; it softened that first blow. Howard looked at his paunchy face in the rear view mirror, and wondered if today he would die.

Tehgan and Jinny were pretty blonde sisters and had been bar staff in the club. Jonah was another student and all night reveller. There had been others in the beginning but Howard never knew their names. Instead he learned quickly how dangerous this new world had become, as one of those sickly, grey things was let inside and swiftly tore the throats out of the funny couple in fancy dress he liked. Rocky Horror to *the horror*. And Howard learned a pool cue could save your life. That left four people. Not one yet twenty one years.

Howard scanned the one way street. His heart sunk when he saw how crammed it was with abandoned cars.

'Hang right, we'll use the pedestrian walkways in the city centre to get through,' Tehgan shouted across. Bodies were everywhere, both dead and undead, and the van started to knock down the walkers like so many bowling pins. The engine revved and protested, but kept making chugging headway.

Howard looked out at the unfolding scene with amazement. This was the furthest they'd ventured since that first morning. The familiar market place, where he'd spent so many afternoons wandering when lectures seemed too much of a chore, was devastated. The glass sliding doors at W H Smith's were wedged open with mutilated dead people. In the gloom of the interior, he could make out the shambling silhouettes of the undead people, drifting between the aisles like rotting ghosts. The water fountain in the centre of the square had run dry, and the circular pool in which it was set teemed with twitching cadavers. In every shop it was the same, densely packed with bodies.

'We have to get out of here Tehgan,' Howard said. In the back, Jonah was crying again and Jinny was trying to hush him.

'Down this road will give us a straight run out of the city and into the country,' Tehgan shouted over, and pointed them the wrong way down a one way street, metal grinding and sparking as the campervan grazed parked cars and walls. The nose of the VW became evermore crumpled as it carved a route through the destruction, and Howard was thankful the engine was in the rear.

It had been Jonah who had made them go, with his incessant talk of disease, typhoid and diphtheria and the like. He had convinced the girls that to stay any longer was tantamount to suicide. *We need to go to country where it's safe,* he'd repeated endlessly. Both sisters had had a crush on him and listened. His athletic toned body had made Howard feel like a sasquatch.

That morning Jonah had run across the street to the campervan in his soldier fancy dress uniform, a size too small for his expansive limbs. There wasn't a zombie in sight. It should have been perfectly safe, but of course, it hadn't been. Howard had watched him yank open the driver door and like a box falling out of a cupboard the child had dropped down. Jonah had managed to push it away, but in the frenzy, the girl found his thigh. Howard and the sisters had rushed to help, and pulled the biting child away. A small cube of flesh hung in her mouth. Howard knew Jonah was as good as dead, *they all did.*

Finally, the city centre was behind them. Howard eased back on the accelerator and glanced back. Already the grey tinge was on Jonah's skin.

'I don't think you can travel any further, buddy. I think we need to drop you off,' Howard said to him. The girls looked shocked but neither said a word.

'You can't do this, man. Don't do it.'

Howard and Jinny lifted him out of the back of the campervan and sat him on the pavement.

'Don't just leave me; I'm begging you, man.'

'We've got to go now. You'll be alright here,' Jinny smiled.

They got back into the van and drove away. Howard watched in the wing mirror as the small figure on the road diminished and then vanished. Tendrils of smoke rose above the ruined city. He was glad they had made it out alive.

The sun went down and the dark proved treacherous. The weak headlights of the aged campervan were near useless at picking out the debris and bodies that littered the country roads.

'We should find a place to stop for the night,' Jinny said.

Half an hour later, they stopped on a road where the trees seemed to bend over like a knotted tunnel, pulling off onto a muddy lay-by. They hadn't seen a moving body for some time and felt they would be safe to rest. In the dim interior light, Tehgan and Jinny set about lighting the single gas hob, while Howard emptied a can of meatballs into a pan.

'Do you think he turned into one of them?' Jinny said as they ate.

Howard could imagine Jonah rising off the pavement and staggering back towards town. His muscled limbs disjointed and disconnected.

'He always loved HMV,' Howard said.

'What?' Tehgan replied.

'Just thinking aloud, wondering where he would have likely wandered off to. That's if he wasn't torn to pieces while he waited for the change.'

'Shut up. That's an awful thing to say. I feel bad enough we had to leave him there,' Jinny said.

'It was either him or us. You should know that,' Howard said. 'I've got a good feeling about this. The zombies are really thinning out. This place you're taking us to Teghan sounds great. I've always loved the sea.'

'We both went there when we were kids. Haven seemed like the quietest place in the world. I think we'll all be really safe there.'

'I hope you're right,' Howard said. Later, when they'd settled into the campervan to sleep he went outside to pee. He shivered with the cold and gazed up at the rustling leaves in the canopy above. In the black, impenetrable woods, he heard twigs creak and snap. Howard wished only animals roamed in the night. Nowhere felt safe anymore.

'How much further do you think?' he said looking at the empty fuel gauge.

'One or two miles. No more than that.' Tehgan frowned, twisting the map round in her hands.

Up ahead, Howard saw the road finally leave the shaded forests and move into open fields and farmland. There was a man trapped on a barbed wire fence with the skin peeling off his body like a burnt baked potato. Howard

108

thought that he must have been set on fire recently. The man struggled more as they passed, reaching out his arms. A silent rage on his putrid lips.

'What the hell is that?' Jinny said.

'Fence of some kind,' Howard replied, stating the obvious. They looked at the high steel fence that seemed to stretch for miles.

'Fucking yes!' Tehgan shouted.

Howard was so busy looking at the fence he almost ran into the man waving at him from next to a quad bike. He looked like a thoroughbred countryman in his green waterproofs and jacket. Howard stopped the van level and could see the man had been working at the engine under the lifted seat. There was a shotgun resting next to his leg.

'Hello folks,' he said cheerily.

'Hello yourself,' Howard replied, trying to stop himself staring at the man's off-centre eyes. 'I'm Howard, and this is Tehgan and Jinny's in the back.'

'Griffin,' the man said. 'Just giving the fuel lead a tweak on this machine here. Great to see some more people. I dare say they'll be plenty of people in the village just dying to hear how things are in the world out there.'

'So there are a lot of survivors in the village then?' Jinny asked.

'A fair few. Not everyone made it you understand, but there's a healthy fifty plus people inside that fence.'

'Great idea by the way.'

'Well thank you ... Howard. Why don't you follow me now and I'll show you the best way in,' he said and started up the quad bike, throwing his tools back onto the holdall on the back.

'What do you think?' Tehgan said to the others. 'You think we can trust crazy eyes?'

'Come on sis, he may look a bit odd but this is our chance to be safe. You really want to go back to that church?'

'So what's it going to be?' Howard said across to Tehgan. Griffin had started beckoning them to follow.

'Okay,' she said. 'Let's do this. The country life here we come!'

Griffin led the van off the road and onto a grassy track and a gap in a dry stone wall. Gradually they went deeper into a copse of trees near the fence line. The trail undulated in and out of trees, before dipping down into a small clearing surrounded by brambles and ferns. Howard looked over at the fence they had followed but couldn't see any opening or gate. Griffin stopped and was walking back towards them. He was motioning Howard to turn off his engine.

'What's up?' he said leaning out of the window. Griffin was looking a little colder now.

'There's still something wrong with my quad bike. I need a bump start. Will you come over and help me?'

'I'm not sure I want to,' Howard mumbled. Something felt wrong, he was sure.

'Come on Howard, the guy's trying to help us here. Don't be a pain,' Tehgan weighed in.

'I just don't want to.'

Griffin opened the driver door and gave him a crooked smile. 'Come on. Girl's calling you a wuss now. Can't have that can we?'

Howard got out. This man just felt all wrong to him. He followed him over to the quad bike.

'Just put your hands on the back and push, okay?'

Howard put his hands on the back, feeling the chipped metal under his fingers. Griffin mounted the bike and Howard pushed, digging his trainers into the soft earth for purchase. The quad bike roared to life and Howard felt a

110

wave of relief. Griffin stepped off again and gave him a hug before walking back towards the campervan. Howard went to follow but suddenly he started to cough and couldn't get enough air into his lungs. A dull ache spread over his side and looking down he saw a dark stain. His legs gave way and he was on his knees.

He tried to wave a warning to the girls but his arms wouldn't obey him. As the light started to fade from his eyes, he saw Tehgan's neck cut wide open and Jinny's kicking heels being dragged away into the trees. Howard thought she was screaming but then the world went inky black.

CHAPTER 18

It was three months down the line and the fence was finished. Summer and I could see it from the upstairs windows of the police station, cutting through the fields ahead of Haven. The village would be safe after all. It felt like the farmers and villagers had done something amazing.

'So what do you want to do today,' I asked and kissed her cherry cheek. Summer blushed so easily.

'Sex and breakfast, and then sex?' she said giggling.

The police station was our home now and the inspector's office had a double bed filling most of the space. If he were alive, I would have loved to see the expression on his face.

Summer and I were a couple. The fence had made us feel like we had some kind of future in a world where the dead waited around every corner to bite and devour.

Later that day we left Lester to his curious experiments and Bill and Arthur to their SKUL work. Those two loved getting their hands dirty, and had an incorrigible enthusiasm for the house clearances. They killed zombies and they killed them well.

I drove out of the station car park and steered towards the beach. No more dead people stumbled over the fields anymore, or lurched in front of my car trying to make me crash. The fence line stretched for over three miles and cocooned the village and many square miles of farmland. We lived in a bubble of England. The walking dead could have everywhere else; we just wanted the space to live our lives.

I chose a different part of the beach to drive to this time, half a mile away from White Creek. I moved the Freelander onto a track made up of two concrete strips in the dirt. The route took us through an abandoned caravan park. The static caravans looked old fashioned and were becoming discoloured by green mosses and lichens. I made a mental note to send in the boys down here for a look-see. You never knew if there would be a lurker or two concealed behind the net curtains in those boxes. I certainly wasn't in the mood for checking today.

Through gaps in the trees, I could see the white shingle pebbles of the beach. Finding the opening, I forced the 4x4 through. We were there. Nothing but cliffs and sand.

'God, it's beautiful,' Summer said.

I followed her gaze; the unnamed bay was shaped like a curve of sloping shingle that led down onto marshy rock pools and the sandy estuary floor beyond. The tide was out and the expanse stretched out for miles across the bay, treacherous due to the quicksands.

In each year I had been a police officer in Haven there had been a death. Usually it was some fool who felt he could cross the bay without help or aid from a trained guide. The sands in the middle would hold feet and then legs in a steel embrace, but it was the tide herself who would deliver the coup de grâce. The fast moving tide would sweep over the poor soul like a miniature tidal wave.

'It's peaceful now the zombies have gone,' I said to her.

'But Johnny they haven't gone anywhere. I've seen them starting to gather against parts of the fence, more every day. They're starting to really scare me.'

'We'll just get those farmers to run them over in their combine harvesters every month. Re-cycle them into fertiliser or something.'

'Ew. Gross, Johnny,' she laughed. 'Come on let's walk.'

We crunched down the shingle banking and onto the beach, looking at the rock pools. It was a beachcomber's paradise down there, assorted treasures mixing in with dark seaweed and crab shells. In the pools, I spotted tiny fish the size of tadpoles, trapped like us in their own little bubble.

We walked around the ragged cliff headland and into the next cove. There on the next beach was a large boat, washed ashore over the last few days since our last visit.

'Come on; let's take a look at this.'

'Are you sure, Johnny?'

We approached it and read the name 'WABBA' on the side. Summer said it was the name of a small furry creature, but I didn't believe her. The shiny blue hull looked intact and the twin outboard engines were impressively robust and powerful. I could see footholds on the back to climb aboard.

'You're not going up there, are you?' she said.

I banged my fist in the hull and a dull noise echoed out.

'I don't think anyone's home.'

'Well, I'm not letting you go in there alone,' she answered.

I started to climb and wobbled with each step. In the bow of the boat, I looked across at the semi-covered cockpit. It appeared remarkably free of the stain and stench of human remains that usually marked everywhere we went these days.

'What do you think?' I whispered.

'I think it looks like we have ourselves a boat to play with.'

I edged up to the plywood door next to the main control panel. Pushing it with one hand, I watched it split down the middle and open like a saloon bar door. The air got suddenly very musty and there was unmistakable waft of decay. Spoke too soon, I thought.

'Wait here.'

'No.'

114

We went down the three steps into the galley of the boat. The room was dim, illuminated only by a short row of round portholes. The kitchen appeared well stocked, with half-sized stainless steel pots and pans that I imagined were unique to boats.

Summer had the hatchet out again, and the mean far away look in her eyes. I pulled at the nearest door and it concertina-ed to one side. In the gloom, I could make out a single cot bed.

'Empty,' I breathed.

The next door was opened by Summer. Inside was a compact toilet. I looked in the bowl and it appeared dried up. One door remained, double sized and at the stern of the boat. We ducked our heads because of the low ceiling and reached out for the handle. The smell was getting rank. I nodded once to Summer and pulled both sides of the door open.

The body was curled into a foetal position at the base of the double bed. The man's skin looked parched and shrivelled, and it was clear that his bodily fluids had semi-evacuated at some point and congealed his remains to the floor like super glue. One blessing was that the guy was fully dead.

'Looks like the captain didn't make it,' I said.

'Let's chuck him onto the beach.'

We rolled him up in the bedding the best we could and wrestled him out of the door. The brown stains had soaked all the way through the mattress, so after we had thrown him on the shingle the bed followed next.

As dusk started to set in, we watched the orange flames dance and rise into the sky. The captain fizzled and spat as the fire took away his diseased flesh.

'It's beautiful out here,' Summer said.

We sat on the shingle with out legs nudged together for warmth, looking out over the expanse of incoming water. Far out to sea I could just make out a red light on the horizon.

'I wonder ...'

CHAPTER 19

The lights strung up in the trees made the farmyard look like Christmas. Soft reggae hummed across the fields as people milled around and talked. Griffin stood behind an industrial sized BBQ doling out lamb and gammon steaks fresh off the grill. Behind him, on the wall, was a poster that read, *'Celebrating the fence, celebrating life.'*

Mark looked at his younger brother and said, 'Dude's definitely not all there. Just look at him. Fucker would pop you on that grill if he had half a chance and turn you into a Macdonald's burger.'

'No, he wouldn't,' Phillip answered. 'Just 'cos you're eleven years old doesn't mean you know everything.' Deep down, Phillip believed him one hundred percent. He didn't even like to look at Griffin and that crazy eye.

They saw their parents beckon them over and they started to weave their way through the sea of people. It seemed funny to Mark that everyone who lived in the village lived here now. The farmhouse was over-crowded, and he hated sharing his room with his parents. He wanted his own room, or at least one to share with Phillip. *So unfair.* He hoped they would move back into their own house now the fence was finished and the dead people were far away.

'Have you boys eaten?' Mrs Hanson said to them.

'We ate earlier and we're not really hungry. Griffin's food is shit anyway,' Mark said.

'No it's not, the lamb is lovely,' Mr Hanson whispered, looking if anybody else had overheard. 'You shouldn't say things like that.'

Mark thought everyone looked really tired, some of them sick almost. Nobody seemed to want to play or have any fun at this party. Everyone had worked all the time on the stupid fence, well everyone but the policeman and his friends. They stayed away and did their own thing. He told his Dad loads of times that they should go and stay with them, but he never wanted to listen. He was glad the fence was finished, he thought, he hoped things would get back to normal now.

A man he knew called Bob Sack came across and started talking to his father. Mark didn't like him either, because he was always sucking up to Jack and Griffin. He thought they must only like him because he was always fixing things around the farm, and up at the windmills that made the electricity. *Fucking brown nose!*

'Mum, can we go and play?' Mark said.

'I don't know, it's getting dark now,' Jean Hanson said.

'They'll be alright. The fence is up and we have no zombies in here anymore. Here's to the fence!' Bob blurted. People around him cheered and raised their glasses as well.

'Okay, boys, just don't leave the farm grounds. No going too far okay?' Toby Hanson said to Mark and Phillip. Mark thought he must be drunk because his nose looked red.

'Okay, we won't,' Mark replied. 'Come on Phillip, let's get out of here.'

They ran past the old barn and headed to the gate behind. He knew the barn was off limits so they didn't linger. It smelled really bad; worse than usual. Mark swore that they'd sneak a look inside one day.

He swung the gate open for his brother, and they were on the track that led to the woods.

'I've got my torch,' Phillip panted, and ran to catch up.

Their feet crunched over the frosty path that led to the edge of the woods. At the end, they had to step over a stile that took them over a stone wall and into the trees. Under the shadow of willows and oaks, it felt to Mark like all the light was suddenly sucked away. Mark stood there silent with Phillip listening. Finally, he said, 'Flick the switch.'

The weak light from the torch lit the trail they walked on. Shiny, slippery limestone poked through everywhere among the loose stones and tree roots, making them both concentrate to keep from stumbling over. The path twisted and contorted the deeper they went into the woods.

'It's so dark, Mark. Are you sure this can't wait until tomorrow?'

'Don't worry, I can see where the path forks. We're nearly there.'

They brushed the over-grown branches and leaves out of their faces, while Mark stared at the ground making sure they didn't lose the path. Out of sight in the dark foliage they heard creatures rustle in the bushes, and above them in a tree an owl hooted. The sound drew their eyes up and through the patchwork canopy of trees they could just make out the faint glow of the moon, peering down like a rheumy eye.

'Did you hear that?' Phillip hissed.

Mark could hear the moaning as well, the sound that was always there like a constant hum behind the fence. The noise the dead people made as they reached out their hands and barged for position behind the fence. Mark hated the way they looked and how they ruined the air so you didn't even want to breathe it in. He also hated when he recognised somebody in the crowd, like the black, eaten face of his old school friend Tim he had seen scrawling along the fence like some rotten slug. That had made him cry to his Mum, then bad dreams ever since.

This sound was different, out there in the black woods was just one dead voice, throwing out its awful howl.

'We should get back,' Phillip said. 'Mum and Dad will be getting so worried. It sounds like there's more one there now.'

'Come on.'

They ducked under a particularly thick branch and suddenly found themselves in a clearing. Mark quickly flashed the torch around to make sure they were in the right place. They were.

The sound again, the hungry wail that speeded down their spine and made their skin shiver.

'I'm scared, Mark.'

'We'll be okay, we've got the fence remember. There can't be anymore of those things in here.'

Mark guided them into the middle of the clearing and shakily started to move the torch beam from tree to tree. Finally, he picked out the man they had come looking for.

'Is he making that sound?' Phillip said as the throaty, gargling mew came again.

Mark edged a little closer. They were approaching the man from the side and the man's face turned away. Mark brought the torch up and shone at the creature's upper body. Mark could see the dark globs of black dotted around its collar, like a necklace of dried blood. Jowls of fat around his neck hung bloated in purple with decay. He had bulbous eyes as if they wanted to pop out of his face. The man was staring right at them.

'I want to go,' Phillip whispered.

'Not yet.'

Mark walked closer to the man who made ugly noises and trashed his head like he was having some fit. Mark stood a foot away, the ripe stench tearing at his nostrils and making him gag. Lowering the torch beam, he could see the rope had ripped a raw trail through the man's wrists and ankles, the binds a dark rouge in colour. The body was tied to the tree and helpless.

'You know what you've got to do,' Mark said to his brother.

'I don't want to do it now.'

'But you've got to.'

Phillip brought the bat down on the man's head and burst it open. His fat head exploded like a smashed watermelon. Bits of his mushy brain fell onto the frosty ground and pooled at their feet.

They'd found him wandering a few days earlier when they'd first sneaked away from the farm when nobody was looking. At first they had run away, scared from the man in the woods, but he had been so slow. They had run circles around him and made a game of it. In the end, it had actually been Phillip who said they wanted to tie it and hurt it, for all the bad things that had happened. Now they had done it, Mark thought.

'Let's get another one soon,' Phillip said.

'Okay.'

CHAPTER 20

Bill steered a police panda car down the rutted track that followed the beach. Arthur sat in the passenger seat studying a torn piece of paper on which Johnny had scrawled a rudimentary map. '*Serious Killing of Undead Life*,' had been Arthur's idea. S.K.U.L. was born out of his love of making up sayings to help him remember things. Arthur chuckled at the thought that he and Bill had come a long way from playing Sudoku in bed on rainy Sunday mornings in their basement flat. He'd lost count now of how many houses they'd cleared, and how many of those rotting things they'd put down.

Arthur glanced onto a back seat dirty with mud and the iron red staining of old blood. On the seat was their arsenal of weapons, which now ranged from machetes to crowbars and sawn-off shotguns. Their favourites were still intact, two thick bladed daggers with white ivory handles. Between them they'd perfected a counter attacking move where a zombie comes forward to be parried and spun just enough for the blade to come crashing through the back of its head. Arthur felt, when he stood side by side with Bill, they were invincible.

The rutted track moved onto two undulating strips of concrete that took them to where the caravans started. Just as Johnny had described, they were crusted with mosses and lichens. Some of them looked like they had been abandoned for years. Arthur started to count the caravans on the left side. This was going to be one of the last SKUL jobs for a long time, retirement beckoned. The houses in the village were all clear, and nobody had reported a zombie loose inside the fence line for weeks. Their work was done, or it had been until Johnny remembered this little caravan park. He had told them, '*why don't you guys go down there and do a little recce and then we'll all go down tomorrow.*' But recces weren't really their style, Arthur knew they were here to do some old fashioned zombie bashing.

'Do you think that's the one?' Bill said.

'That's the one,' Arthur replied. He could see the grand lace curtains. *It had to be.*

They flung the grubby florescent police stab-proof vests over their heads and pulled the heavy leather gloves on. Bill and Arthur went instinctively for the daggers, and then smiled and swapped when they realised they'd picked each others up. Taking some deep breaths Arthur went up to the side window with a torch. The static caravan was on blocks too high to look in directly, so he stood on a large plant pot and wobbled.

Arthur shone the torch into the murk and started to make out various objects inside. The window looked into the lounge area with a pull-out table, the cushions on the semi-circle of seating were dislodged and on the floor. Some food was on the table, and the floor had all the tell tale signs of a massive disturbance, with cutlery and glass smashed all over the brown carpet. Arthur moved the torch beam further into the caravan, and could see the pine doors on the wall cupboards broken and crushed. From his experience, he knew there must be something inside, another body that needed its end.

Arthur pushed the torch beam a little further and started to see into the kitchen area. He found it difficult to see any further, and pushed his face against the clear plastic window. Arthur could just make out some open drawers and a mess of utensils on the nearest side board. There was something else as Arthur squinted into the gloom. There was a brown shiny shoe behind an open cupboard. It was right at the back of the caravan. He couldn't make it out very clearly. Then the shoe moved.

'SHIT!' he shouted, as the plant pot collapsed and he fell onto his back. Arthur was winded, trying to gasp for breath that wouldn't come.

'Are you okay down there, mate?' Bill said smiling.

'Can't bree ...' came out as a faint whisper. Then all at once, he saw it. There was a woman crawling out from underneath the caravan. Bill had his back to her, and was bending down to help him. Slow motion almost, she was tearing into Bill's exposed calf muscle with a dirty, soil-filled mouth. Bill screamed and the sound broke Arthur's heart.

Arthur felt his vision begin to fray around the edges, starved of oxygen. The pressure built up in his diaphragm and finally his lungs sprang back to life again. Deep breaths at last, when the caravan door burst open and the thing with the shoes was coming at him. Arthur scratched blindly in the dirt for his dagger, but the ruin of a man crushed him under his weight. The precious air was forced out again, and bile rose up in his mouth.

Above him were pitiless rotting eyes and a skull-face dry and mummified. The world was fading again, and Arthur felt the thing tear away his ear, making his head ring. He looked over towards where Bill lay. The brown soil was swimming red in his blood. The woman was eating greedily around the useless stab vest. Already he could see he was twitching and convulsing, the change was happening fast.

Arthur went to push the man away from his neck, but then stopped himself. He just wanted to be with Bill. They would dead walk together in this next life.

Soulmates forever.

CHAPTER 21

Jean Hanson let out another awful cry, 'OOOWWWW!' The faces around her in the bedroom looked blank, fearful.

'How long is it since the last contraction?' shouted Toby Hanson, barrelling his way back into the room, hands full of towels and a kettle of boiled water. 'Does any one know where the painkillers are? I've checked the kitchen and they're gone.'

'You'll be okay, won't you Mum,' said Mark. His younger brother Phillip was silent, cheeks burnt red by the tears. Their Mum looked so sick and weak propped up on the double bed. Her face was beetroot red and the bulge of her stomach looked impossibly big.

'OOOWWWW!'

Toby looked out of the farmhouse window for some inspiration. The situation had caught them by surprise. They had counted and were sure the baby wasn't due for weeks. One minute they had been making a bath up and the next this. That bastard Jack had done nothing to help, the man had disappeared out into the fields with his degenerate son for the day and taken most of the villagers with them. Alison tore into the room.

'Thank God,' Toby gushed.

'Listen boys, your Mum needs some time and space to have this baby. I bet you can't wait to see if it's a little brother or sister,' she said, hustling them out. 'I'll be back in a tick.'

Toby squeezed his wife's hand. "We'll get through this, just you watch.'

'OOOWWWW!'

He grabbed one of the white towels and started to dab off the perspiration from Jean's forehead. Toby kept looking down the bed at her bare legs and the stain on the linen her waters had made. How long had they until the baby came? He picked up the tattered library book he'd found in the village, *How to Give Birth* by Karen Waldron. Over twenty five years old, he flicked it open and ten pages detached from the spine and fell onto the floor.

'Fuck it,' he hissed, and scooped them up. He felt like he was starting to lose it.

'The boys are fine, sorted them out with a nice big jigsaw. Now where are we?' Alison said from the door.

'It. Hurts. Too. Much.'

'Look we'll get through this. We've just got to stay calm. Childbirth is the naturalest thing in the world. You'll see,' Alison said. 'Right, let's take a look.'

Alison went down and parted Jean's legs. 'Look this may smart a bit, but I need to reach in there and see how far off you are.'

'So you were a nurse right, back before all this happened,' Toby whispered to Alison.

'Not exactly, but my sister was a community midwife. She used to tell me all the old war stories and gory details. I've got a fair mind what to do down there. Piece of cake, trust me,' she said raising her voice. 'Now you stay calm and still, okay Jean? This won't take a second.'

'OOOWWWW!'

'Okay, I'm estimating her cervix is nearly fully dilated. That's pretty damn far gone missy. It's just a matter of time now. Toby, go to my dresser will you? First drawer down on the right and you'll find a small tub of aspirin. Not great, but better than nothing for your pain.'

An hour later and Jean was screaming and crying. Her hands had torn shreds out of the sheets on both sides of the bed. The linen was running freely with her blood.

'You gotta push like hell, honey. I can see its head now,' Toby shouted.

'Come on, it's crowning. We're nearly there, just a few more minutes. Let me just get these gloves on to catch the baby,' Alison added.

There was a rush of movement and in a blur, there was a new born baby on the dirty linen sheets. Wet crimson viscera splattered off the bed and onto the polished floor. The baby lay prone. Silence edged round the room. Alison lifted it up and wrapped it in a towel. The cord arced down, still bonding mother to child.

'She's beautiful,' Alison said, shakily.

Jean looked over with her tired eyes and tried to focus. Something wasn't right. The room started to spin a little and she concentrated hard to make it stop. 'What's happening? Make her cry. Why's she not crying?'

'Jesus, she is turning blue. Do something, Alison. Come on, hurry up,' Toby said, snatching up the baby.

'I think it's the cord, we need to cut the cord,' Alison said, reaching for the scissors.

'Jesus, how can it be the cord? She's not breathing. Can you do mouth to mouth?' Toby shouted.

'Just let me do this, alright,' Alison said and made the snip. 'Hold this end.'

Toby looked horrified as dark liquid started flowing through both the baby's cut cord and Jean's. He pinched his fingers over the baby's cord and shouted, 'Get some fucking string.'

The baby's face was not just blue, but bright blue as if she had blue blood flowing in those tiny veins. Toby started blowing tiny puffs of air into her mouth, and watched her little rib cage rise and fall. The baby's arms and legs were limp, her head lolling lazily back against his arm.

'My baby ...' Jean cried from the bed. There was no response. She wanted to sleep now. She wanted this all to be a dream that would go away. The room was silent again, then filled by Jean's piercing howl, 'MY BABY GIRL!'

'Let me try,' said Alison.

The poor nameless baby girl was passed back and forth, never moving. Finally, Toby laid her down in the cot he had built in the corner of the room; his eyes welling up when he saw his wife holding the child to her breast, trying to feed it better. Detached and floating, he felt his mind clamping down on his emotions. He hated this world.

Soon, the fatigue overtook Jean and she slept, the baby limp in her arms still. The bottom of the bed was awash with blood and afterbirth, but he didn't suppose it really mattered.

'Listen, Jack and the others will be back soon. I should go and make a start with dinner. I'll come and help with whatever you need later. Perhaps we could have a proper burial or a funeral ... I could talk to Jack,' Alison said. 'I'm just so sorry.'

'You did everything you could. You've nothing to be sorry about,' Toby said flatly, pushing past her onto the landing. He heard someone creaking their way up the steep staircase and walked over to see who it was.

Griffin.

'So have you finished making fucking babies,' he sneered.

Toby punched him on the side of the head. He didn't even realise he was doing it until it was done. It was as if his subconscious had taken over and sent his hand out to do some business. *And Business was good!* Griffin tumbled back down the staircase, like an old black and white Laurel and Hardy sketch. The shocked impression on Griffin's face was priceless.

'You broke my fucking arm,' Griffin shouted back, his left arm grotesquely bent back at the elbow. Snapped like a twig.

'Daddy,' Phillip said from behind him. 'What did you do?'

And then, like the onset of a hurricane, reality came flooding back.

What did I do? he thought.

CHAPTER 22

'Where are they?' I said for at least the fifth time since Summer, Lester and I had left the station.

'They said they were going check out the caravans, I told you that was all Arthur and Bill told me.' Summer's nose wrinkled when she was mad, and her cheeks blushed a fierce red.

Lester sat in the back of the 4x4, a heavy crow bar on his lap. He was clearly under no illusion that Bill and Arthur's failure to return for twelve hours could only be likely to be bad.

Very bad.

I stopped the Freelander a short distance from the caravan. The PVC door was flapping open in the breeze, and the ground was littered with rubbish. When we stepped out and looked more closely, there was no doubt that there had been a life and death struggle. Fresh blood stained the earth; lashings of it.

'What happened?' Summer said, as much to herself as us. She knew.

'Look, we make a quick search and we head back. It's getting dark and it's clearly not safe around here,' I said.

'Johnny, look out!' Lester shouted.

I turned around to see a grey hand reaching out and grabbing for my ankle. From the shadow of the crawl space beneath the static caravan, I could make out the outline of a withered face, all cheekbone and teeth. Pulling my leg away, I felt the thing's dirty nails scrape my skin with preternatural strength. Summer was at my side, and with one slashing movement had her hatchet in its wrist. The blade went in deep, if not all the way through. Underneath the bone looked yellow and fetid.

Lester didn't waste time. The pointed end of his crowbar went in through the eye socket of the under-dweller with a dry *pop*. 'You were right Johnny,' he said with a smile. 'It clearly isn't safe.'

'Are you okay?' Summer asked, her hands on my trouser leg.

'No harm done,' I said. The nails hadn't gone through the canvas material, but the skin above my ankle had angry red rake marks. The truth was I pretty shaken. I just wanted to get back to the safety of the station. 'Come on, a quick search and let's get the fuck out of here.'

My head poked through the doorway of the caravan. There was a stench of decay in there, and everything that wasn't broken was over-turned. I guessed the partner of the thing under caravan had been trapped here since the outbreak, getting very hungry. Then one fine day Bill and Arthur had come along and let it out. Shuddering, I kicked myself for even thinking that there were any safe places in this world now. The fence had made us all soft. I felt like I was losing my nerve.

'I shouldn't have let them go anywhere alone.'

'It wasn't your fault,' Summer said. Her hand squeezed mine.

'Come on,' Lester said. 'We need to get a move on. The light's fading and there could be three bodies out here somewhere. We'll warn the farm and come back tomorrow in force. Nothing we can do now, Johnny.'

'Looks that way,' I said walking back to our vehicle.

We drove out of the caravan park, and didn't plan to come back in a hurry. I didn't want to think how many more hungry mouths might be dormant in the endless rows of mouldering caravans. As the dusk came, and the yellow ball of light slipped deep into the tree line, I wondered if a person's courage could suddenly run out. As a group we had felt strong for a time. Clearing houses full of the dead, perhaps all we'd ever had was luck. The world was an unfathomable and dangerous place all over again. I just wanted to hole up in the station and never come out.

Summer must have read it on my face, because she said, 'Don't worry, it's just the shock. Look, I'll drive us.'

When we broke out onto the beach road again, I looked out at the pebble beach and the quicksands beyond and wanted to see them. I don't mean the romantic notion of seeing Bill and Arthur in one piece after what we'd seen at the caravan, clearly that was never going to happen. Part of me wanted to see those bodies out there on the sands and exposed. I wanted to walk right up and look into the dead faces of my former friends. I wanted to put them down, and kill the nightmares that I knew were coming. But the sands were empty apart from the fat seagulls, and there was no quick fix for me. They were inside the fence line someplace, and they meant to haunt all my days and nights to come.

'Look,' said Summer. 'I know that kid, he's from one of the families at the farm.' I looked up from my stupor just as we turned into the police station car park. I sped up and parked the Freelander in front of him. *What the hell?* He looked completely terrified.

Mark was shouting through my door window before I'd even turned the engine off.

'They won't stop hurting him. They won't stop hurting my dad.'

CHAPTER 23

'You're crazy,' Summer told me again. 'This plan, if you could even call it that, is going to get you killed.'

'No, it's not,' I said. We'd brought Mark into our refreshment room at the station and he was greedily wolfing down some of Lester's fabled chilli. The lad looked tired and cold. He'd told us how scared everyone was of Jack and Griffin at the farm, and how his Dad had lashed out at Griffin. Things had gotten a whole lot worse, off the scale worse. I kicked myself for not realising earlier.

'Just stay here, okay? And look after the boy. I'll handle this,' I said to Summer, buttoning up my work shirt and fixing on a black clip on tie.

'I'm not staying with that boy. Lester can do that fine. I am going with you. This stupid plan will work better with two people anyway.'

'I'd go with the flow if I was you, son,' Lester piped in. 'You're not going to win with this one.'

I waited for Summer to dig out her old PCSO uniform from a bottom drawer.

'Never thought I'd be wearing this again.'

On the way out of the door I stopped. 'We need our hats. Full uniform will help us pull this off.'

'Sure Johnny, hats will make all the difference,' Summer smiled.

The drive to the farm was a lot quicker than it used to be now there weren't bodies cluttering up the roads. The drop down the valley gave a clear view of the fence that bisected the series of fields to the east of the village. From this distance, it looked like ants were gathering in their hundreds on the other side. Except they weren't ants, they were the rotting, stinking, walking carcasses. A festering reminder of our bubble, and the fact that everywhere else belonged now to the dead. I wanted to get used to the way things were, but it just never happened.

'More everyday,' Summer said.

Nodding, I steered the police vehicle down the gravel track towards the farm. They had some new building project underway; a crude breezeblock framework that appeared to be some new accommodation block being built next to the farmhouse. It was a total eyesore, but who cared about these things anymore, I told myself. Planning permission was just two redundant words.

I parked and killed the engine. Curious faces of the villagers were coming out to have a look-see. Lester, Summer and I often talked over sambuca shots about how we felt like outsiders in the village. What made us not want to be part of this farm community? I liked Summer's answer best, she hated the smell of shit in the morning and thought cows' big, glassy eyes were pure evil.

'I haven't seen you two down here in over a month. What's with the uniforms?' Bob Sack said poking his fat face through the driver window.

'Official business I'm afraid. How are those wind turbines?'

'You know, still turning.' He looked a little confused. Worry lines breaking out on his forehead.

Summer and I stepped out of the vehicle and we started walking towards the farmhouse.

'Where are you going? Jack and Griffin aren't far away you know. Chasing down those two zombie poofters, no doubt.'

'Anyone seen them yet?' Summer asked.

'No, nobody's seen a thing. Maybe they just crawled off and died,' Bob said with an awkward skip to get in front of us. 'Look I really don't think you should go inside. Just wait until Jack and Griffin get back okay.'

'Can't do that,' I said in my best police tone. 'Crime scene. Can't lose any more evidence.'

I pushed past, and Summer followed close behind. I saw the woman I knew as Alison tidying away washed pots and pans in the kitchen. I looked her straight in the eyes and gambled.

'Can you show me the stairs where it happened? We need to see it straight away.'

Alison hesitated a beat. 'Of course, right this way.'

Bob Sack was still protesting, but I could see Alison was on side and happy to play along. Summer and I knew there was an inherent ridiculousness in what we were doing, but we were going to play it straight for all it was worth.

'It happened right there,' Alison said pointing to a series of broken banister rails on the stairs.

'I'm going to get Jack and Griffin right now. Jesus, you haven't even asked how Griffin is yet. He's the victim after all, isn't he?' Bob said, heading for the front door.

'Of course he is,' Summer said, giving her sweetest smile.

Once he was out of the way, I turned to Alison.

'Look, we haven't got much time. We need to get Jean and Toby, and their son Phillip out of here and to the police station. Mark told us what they were doing to Toby, and unless you want to be implicit in a murder, you've got to help us. Where are they?'

'Mrs Hanson and Phillip are locked in their room. Mr Hanson is out in the back yard. You need to help him quickly, before it's too late.' Alison replied.

'Okay, Alison you go with Summer and help get Jean and Mark to our vehicle. I'll get Toby.'

Turning, I walked swiftly through the house. Gathering voices were clearly audible at the front of the farmhouse. I weaved my way through the back rooms, and stepped through the glass-panelled door into the back yard.

The walled garden was empty, nothing but clothes on a washing line and broken rabbit hutches. There were two sheds next to a high dry stone wall. Inside were a rusted lawnmower and other long ceased machinery. I waded deeper into the overgrown brambles and found a vague outline of a path.

At the far end was a man hung by his hands from the outstretched branches of a willow tree. No boxer would've been allowed to take the punishment visible in his face. One eye was swollen as if a ripe plum was growing out of the socket. His gagged mouth was a bloodied mass of broken teeth and torn gums. Long strips of flesh had been flayed off his torso. One arm was dislocated and clearly broken. This was revenge to the power of ten.

'Toby, can you hear me?'

His head lolled back. In his good, eye a series of rapid blinks.

He was alive.

My knife came out of my back pocket, and I gently cut the bindings. He immediately slumped into my arms, heavy and wheezing.

'You need to stand up, you've got to try. We need to walk out of here Toby, or neither of us will make it,' I said pulling the gag out of his mouth.

'My family ... you have to save them first. Please.'

'They are fine,' I said. 'Alison is taking them to my police car right now. Jean and Phillip are fine. Mark is already at the station. He's the one who told me what these bastards were up to. Come on Toby, we need to get going.'

I half steered, half dragged him back into the farmhouse. In the kitchen, I saw some people from the village. They didn't say anything, and wouldn't meet my eyes. Ashamed, they didn't offer any help either. We made it all the way to the front door and we staggered out into the farmyard.

Shit!

'Well officer, what have you got yourself there,' Jack sneered.

'Come into my Dad's house without asking first will you. Tut! Tut!' Griffin added. He had his left arm crudely splinted between two sticks of wood. A shotgun leaned against his leg.

Jack and Griffin had positioned themselves in front of the Freelander. Alison, Jean and Phillip were stood with Summer to one side.

'Jesus Christ,' Jean cried, and ran over to where I was holding her husband upright. 'What have they done to you?'

'Can you hold him one minute?' I whispered to her.

Walking forward, all eyes fell on me. The other villagers hovered on the periphery of the yard. It was time to make my six years feet dragging through a police career finally count for something. There was more than one life to save now. I held my breath until I was within two feet of Jack, then spoke.

'So Jack, I hear you've been having yourself a few issues lately.'

'If you call that fucker cold cocking my son and breaking his arm issues, then yes you're right. Got what was coming to you, didn't you Toby. Not half finished yet neither.'

'We've got a crime here Jack, there is no getting away from that,' I spoke up, clear and loud.

'Our officer here standing in his bright sparkling uniform seems to be failing to remember the world ain't what it was. We got five hundred head of zombie behind that fence line. Ain't no government paying you wages. World turned to shit, or didn't you notice?' Griffin spat at me. 'We do our own justice now.'

'The fuck you do Griffin,' I said. 'You think just because you built a bit of fence you are suddenly above the law. What do you think would happen if the army came into town tomorrow, and they found out you'd killed a man? Not a zombie, but an innocent man, Griffin, what do you think they would do with you?'

'Fucking army? Ain't nobody here but us.'

'You sure of that? You looked further than the end of your nose? When did you last take a ride out to the cities? And what about the other countries? Truth is we don't know shit. So maybe you two should think on. Until we know any different, I think you might want to restrain yourself from killing every person that looks at you cross-eyed.'

'Are you coming to a point somewhere in that horse shit?' Jack snarled.

'Now, there has been a crime committed here, and it's my duty to investigate. That's my fucking job, wages or no wages. So Mr Hanson here is coming to the station to answer some questions. And Phillip and Jean are coming too. They're material witnesses, and I want their statements.'

'No fucking way. They stay,' Griffin shouted in my face.

'You know how this ended last time,' I reminded him.

'Try it again. Make my damn year.'

'Hold your fucking water Griffin,' Jack snapped. 'Anyways, I'm curious to see what the officer's idea of justice is anyhow.'

I took my chance and beckoned Summer and Jean to come forward. I looked at Alison, asking her with my eyes if she wanted to come too. She just slunk back in the shadows of the porchway. Too scared, I imagined.

Pushing past Jack, I opened up the vehicle. All the time I was terrified Griffin might open up the shotgun and kill us where we stood. I gestured to Summer and got us and the Hansons into the vehicle as quickly as possible. Jack was gesturing for me to roll the window down.

'Don't think I don't know what you're doing. I thought I'd give you a free pass this time, purely for my amusement,' Jack said leaning in. 'Next time you go in my house uninvited, I got a nice patch of honeysuckle bush I'm going to bury you under. We clear?'

'Crystal,' I said and drove away.

'We're going to have to watch our backs now,' I said to Summer.

She nodded.

'We should leave this place soon. All of us.'

CHAPTER 24

'You know I remember you now,' Jean Hanson said as we made the upstairs sergeant's room back into a habitable living space.

'I interviewed Phillip and Mark for burning all those rubbish bins in the village. Big case for me,' I laughed.

'You were pretty decent, I thought,' Jean replied. 'I take it you don't really want to interview me for Griffin's arm?'

'Tape machine broke last year anyway, and they never replaced it. Seriously, I may have to think up something to keep those psychos happy. Community service maybe? Let me think on it, and I'll come up with something.'

'You're a good man.'

Toby Hanson slept on the mattress we'd put down on the floor of the office. He had been catatonic all the journey back, and was yet to say a word. I suspected we might lose him, that his injuries were far beyond recoverable with our primitive medical skills. It wasn't hard to read Jean's face. She must have been thinking the exact same thing. Every one of us knew how it was to lose people. This world was nothing but grief and loss and murder. I knew that even before the outbreak came.

'I'm going to stay with him a while,' Jean said. 'Will you make sure Phillip and Mark don't do anything stupid, like burn the place down?'

'Not much to burn now, after Lester took his turn. You lost your child at the farm. Are you sure you are alright, that you don't need anything?,' I asked.

'Got a time machine perhaps?' Jean replied, turning her face away.

I found Summer and Lester in the refreshment room. She was whipping up some powdered Angel Delight for the two young boys, who sat at the table with sporks in their hands. They couldn't get enough of the stuff.

'How are we all doing?' I said trying to keep it upbeat. 'Where's that old bird Jefferson got to now? He was here a minute ago.'

'Out for another walk,' Lester said, looking up from one of the old newspapers he liked to collect. 'Old buzzard walks more miles than a damn postman. Said he wanted to take another look around for Bill and Arthur.'

'Hope he took his pistol,' Summer added. 'I'm sick of everyone dying around here.'

'No-one's dying,' I said back to her and nodded at the boys. 'Let's keep it upbeat okay.'

'Food's getting a little on the low side. With our new guests it might be best if we get down that supermarket and do some digging,' Summer said closing up the freezer.

'Well, it's something to do. Professor Lester, are you game to join me?' I said.

'Most certainly.'

'I'll look after these two mud scrappers,' Summer said.

I looked across and watched Phillip and Mark devouring their Angel Delight. *Not a care in the world.* It was good to see.

I fired the Freelander down the hill to the main row of shops in the village. There was a spoken agreement with the farmers that only tinned or packet food that was needed would be taken. Stocks were low, but usually there was always stuff to be found on the shelves or the store rooms at the back. I parked in a space outside the old green grocers, a place that was nothing but rotten, pulped vegetables and awful odours. The Village Store was next door. It looked like we had the place to ourselves.

The Store was larger and better stocked than Tomlinson's on the hill, and after my bad experience on the first day of the outbreak I much preferred going to this place. It was brighter, and the aisles were much wider. It just felt an all-round safer bet.

Lester and I entered cautiously, my hands gripping the sawn-off tight enough to turn my knuckles white. We knew short, fast response weapons were by far the best idea in these confined spaces. Going up the aisle Lester grabbed a basket. There were a lot of bare spaces on the shelves now. I found some corned beef, pasta, powdered milk and cereal.

'I'm starting the vegetable garden up in the summer. Some rich guy's lawn is going to get turned into an allotment. I'm telling you, Johnny, either we go Good Life or we perish.'

'Does that make you Felicity Kendall then, Lester?'

'Always cracking the wise, aren't you.'

'I'm sorry Lester. You're right of course. You've come a long way from those streets, do you know that?' I picked up a jar of olives, and then sat them back down again.

'Yeah, and you've come a long way from being a fascist with a tit hat too,' he smiled.

'You know Lester, I've remember picking up a swab of something chemical back on the first day this happened. It was the strangest thing, the water was almost sparkling around this dead seal. If I can find it, perhaps we could take a look at it together.'

Lester smiled again. He no longer looked anything like the drunken tramp with a chip on his shoulder. There was a deep scholarly feel about him now. He'd even taken to wearing a casual suit and tie. Only in a certain light could you see the wear and tear on his skin, from the cold nights sleeping rough with only a bottle of the cheap stuff for company.

'You've done well, you know that. What's your secret?'

'I don't know. I guess this new world has given me a second chance. Back in the day, I burnt too many bridges to ever get back into society. Here, I feel I might be able to save the whole world. It feels better than drinking somehow,' he said.

'Does that make me your sponsor?'

We drove away with our meagre rations, enough food for another week at least. At the station I saw Summer standing outside, looking up at the building. There was worry on her face.

'Somebody broke our window. They threw this,' she said holding up a half brick.

CHAPTER 25

We should have felt safe with a fence cutting us off from the dead. There should have been a feeling of community, of massive collective gratitude that we'd all survived against the odds. But it wasn't like that now, and it probably never was. Jack and Griffin ran the farm, and the villagers were their new livestock. People bent to their will as if the trauma of the outbreak had robbed them of their own free will. It appeared that only a few villagers, such as the Hansons could see past the dictatorship and try to break away. For the rest, the need to survive the apocalypse by whatever means overrode their moral codes and value systems. At least the dead were honest, they just wanted to eat you every time.

'PIGS END'

As I looked up at red painted graffiti scrawled over my beloved Freelander it felt as rotten in this so-called bubble as beyond the fence line. That morning I'd seen things that had been human stood reaching through metal links, with rats living in the empty cavities where their stomachs should be. Vermin as parasitic house guests in people's own bodies. I wished I could feed Jack and Griffin to them.

'What do you want to do?' Summer asked me.

'If we go there and confront them with no evidence, we'll get nowhere fast. Short term it would be better to catch them at it. Take turns on look out, maybe rig up a camera.'

'And long term?'

'Get the hell out of here.'

It had been weeks since the first window had been broken. Since then other small things had been broken or gone missing. It was subtle, and it was not every day, but beneath it I suspected something of a campaign against us. We'd see Griffin drive past and wave far more regularly then before with some minion or other. We would have to be blind not to see he was sending us a message. Whispers came that he was bitter. His broken arm had healed badly. Griffin hated that we had taken Toby Hanson out of his reach. It was clear he wasn't ready for anything approaching bygones or forgiveness.

I'd mentioned the words *'community service'* to Jack in the days after taking the Hansons away from the farm, aiming to placate him somehow. Jack had dismissed me with the words, 'Justice will be here soon enough.' He told me not to worry about that, 'That a time was coming.' Looking into his cold, glassy eyes that day I realised we were all basically fucked.

'We should check on Toby,' Summer said. We'd stared enough at the graffiti.

Upstairs in the station you could smell Toby. Not the rot of the dead, but the musty reek of somebody who hadn't left his room, let alone his bed, in over three weeks. Summer and I checked on him from time to time, but in the main we left his care to his Jean.

The brutal injuries remained, the healing process inhibited by poor medicines and medical knowledge, compounded by our survivor's diet. His shattered arm was the biggest concern. Too many fragments for even a jigsaw master to put right, we'd encased it in a mess of metal bars and papier mache cement. We gave him every antibiotic and painkiller we could find in the village. Toby's hand and fingers still went black, and he still moaned and writhed constantly in his sleep. Never to wake, never to be whole again.

Lester said he thought the arm should come off, but even the mad scientist didn't have the heart for such a doomed operation. Toby's face was a mash of crude stitches, Summer's best work holding together what was left of a family man tortured into this near unrecognisable monster. Gouges in the body were covered with oozing, dirtied gauzes, hiding a multitude of wounds that refused to close or heal.

'How long?' Summer asked me as we hovered near the door, both of us spying through a porthole window. Jean knelt on the mattress, dabbing a wet cloth on the bare skin of her husband, trying to chase another fever away.

'Not long,' I said. The inevitable could not be postponed forever.

Later, after we had eaten, Jefferson stood next to the half open window. 'So dark tonight, no stars. The clouds are smothering up the sky.'

'Good,' Summer said. 'It might keep us a little warmer.'

Jefferson gave a little chuckle then. His slight old man's frame had something of a pixie look about it.

'Where do you go on all those walks, Jefferson?,' I said.

'I'm just a simple man Johnny. Walks take me out of my head for a little while. Stop me thinking too much about those things behind the fence. No big mystery there.'

'But you're the most mysterious person I know,' laughed Summer.

Afterwards, Summer and I laid back on our bed and talked in the dark. It was soothing just to talk, two discombobulated voices in the inky black, drifting towards sleep.

'I don't remember him you know,' Summer said.

'Remember who?'

'Jefferson. In all my time walking through the village, all those community meetings, I never saw him. What about you?'

'You're right, I never saw him either. Strange ...' I said, and sleep took me in her warm embrace.

Waking with a start, I heard muffled voices and then the unmistakable sound of the front door slamming shut. Still groggy, I staggered to the office window and looked down. Under the dark shadow of the houses opposite I made out the silhouette of Jefferson walking away. I felt annoyed because he had promised to do a whole night shift on look-out. And now there he was walking away. *Always with the walking.* There would be words said later.

Then I heard a second sound. A creaking on the floor boards, a stutter-step on the stairs. Somebody was moving on the ground floor, and now up the stairs. I went for my jeans out of modesty, and the delay saved my life. By the time I got out of our bedroom the zombie had already lurched into the Hanson's room.

What happened next was a blur of movement and screams. I shouted a warning for Summer and fumbled for the corridor light. *Click*, then nothing. The fuse box must have tripped again. Another scream, this time it was Jean and the boys together. A cacophony of fear and anger, trapped and scared out of their minds.

'GET AWAY FROM US!'

The floor of our bedroom was littered with four, maybe five weapons hidden in the blackness. Summer and I fumbled for something to use, anything. In the dark panic and adrenalin rush our hands kept coming up empty. Finally I found a machete handle. Summer had something smaller. I guessed it could only be her beloved hatchet.

Running blind into the Hanson's room I could make out a bundle of shapes against the outline of the mattress on the floor. Between the screams was the low bass sound I'd heard too many times, the sound of feasting, raw muscle and tendon being torn free from the living. My eyes

147

adjusted enough to make out friend from foe. The body had gone for the easy meat of the comatose Toby, broken and dying, but still enough to excite the dead palate. Jean who had tried to stop it, had got in the way, and now her leg was being ripped to the bone. Blood streaked the floor like an abattoir.

Phillip and Mark bolted past me and away into the corridor. They had seen enough, and I was glad they were safe. Summer and I stepped forward. She buried the hatchet with precision deep into the back of the body's neck. The creature looked up, confused but still aware. Its shadowy, rotting face turned to me and tried to rise. My blade swept down and cleaved its head in two. It split like a rotten coconut, the stench overwhelming.

Jean Hanson lay there panting, her arms wrapped around her husband. The tube lights flickered back into life on the ceiling. Blinking I looked over the scene in front of me, as Lester burst into the room.

'I knocked the fuse box switches back into place ... Jesus,' he said.

Mrs Hanson's leg was a ruin. At the bottom of the open wound I could see the white of her femur. Nearby, the zombie's mouth was crammed with raw meat, like the end of a butcher's mincing machine. The wet sheen was on Jean's skin already, and the vacant look in her eyes meant her change was coming fast.

'We need to ...' I started to say, but Summer finished my sentence. Not with any words, but with her hatchet cracking down twice on Jean's skull. She looked across at Toby too, slowly dying of gangrene or whatever blood infection was slowly killing him. Oblivious to everything that had happened. She glanced back at me for an answer, her blue eyes half crazed, half resigned to it all.

'Leave him, I can't see a bite,' I said. The murder might have been a kindness, but it was Summer who would have to live with it, and carry its burden. Summer was all I had, she couldn't break.

The hatchet dropped and she held me; a deep sob against my ribs.

'It will be alright.'

'The switches were all flicked back,' Lester said. 'On the fuse box. Every one.'

I tried to make some sense of what he was saying. In the refreshment room I could hear Phillip and Mark crying.

'It's Jefferson,' I said at last. 'I think Jefferson is a traitor.'

CHAPTER 26

At first light we carried Jean Hanson's body the far end of the car park and set it alight next to the other body. The flames on her skin licked orange and yellow. I was glad Phillip and Mark were asleep, exhausted in mine and Summer's bed. There was no ceremony of words from the bible, we had more immediate concerns. It was not enough that the dead walked the earth, it appeared the survivors wanted us dead as well.

'Are you sure it was the farmers?' Summer said quietly as we watched the pyre die down.

'How could it not be?'

Half an hour later and Summer and I sat in the 4x4. I knew we needed to see Jack, and his bastard son Griffin before things really got out of hand.

'Are you sure this is a wise idea?' Lester said through my rolled down driver's window. 'I mean, I've had my differences down the line with officers of the law. But Johnny, I'm the only person around here bar those damn crazy farmers that actually half-like this new world. And I like you being in that world, Johnny. Don't go getting yourself and beautiful Summer here killed for no reason.'

'We'll be okay. I just need to have a word with them, and see if we can't find some compromise. I mean, maybe Jefferson was just a crazy coot after all, and it has nothing to do with Jack and Griffin.'

'I don't have the answer to that conundrum, unfortunately. I do know old Jefferson's room has been left neat as a pin. Fucker must have been sneaking his stuff away over the last few days when we weren't looking. I don't think he'll be back anytime soon. It has me worried, Johnny. Last night seemed pretty pre-planned to me,' Lester said. 'Just take care alright. I don't want to go back to living on my own anytime soon.'

'No worries, Lester,' Summer said from the passenger seat. 'Any hostility and we're straight back here. Promise.'

We took our time on the drive towards the farm. From the high vantage point before the road wound down I could see the crowds of dead. Too many bodies down there to count now, crawling over each other like the bugs they were. The fence couldn't hold forever. My eyes flicked across to the woods to my right. I felt paranoid that people from the farm were watching us, expecting us.

I was right.

'Jesus, what the hell are they doing?' Summer said squirming in her seat.

Ahead, the road was blocked. A horse box was sideways in the road. There was barbed wire and sandbags. Bob Sack had a rifle in his hands. Two other men stood next to him, guns in their hands too.

I stopped the Freelander a good seventy metres from where they waited for us. I figured if they were going to start shooting, at least the range would make it difficult.

'Wait here,' I said.

'What?'

'Wait here, I want to talk to them,' I said sharply.

'Okay,' Summer said. She was as scared as me.

I walked the distance between the 4x4 and where they stood. I felt exposed, like a man walking towards a firing squad. The morning air was crisp, biting at my skin.

'Bob,' I said. 'Have you joined Dad's Army?'

Bob didn't laugh. He looked pained, his round face a picture of turmoil. 'Look Johnny, I've got my orders.'

'What have they told you to do?' I said, my palms clammy.

'Nobody comes in anymore.'

'Is that it, Bob? You know if you shoot me I'll just come back as a ghost and haunt you forever.'

'Don't be daft,' Bob said. Half a smile.

'Can I speak to you alone for a second,' I said, drawing Bob away from the two goons he was stood with. 'What can you tell me about Jefferson?'

Bob paused for thought. Sweat globules standing out on his forehead. 'He's down there on the farm. Good friend of Jack's.'

I looked down towards the farmyard that was more like a building site; villagers industrious worker bees on the new accommodation block. I couldn't see the traitor.

'That's all I wanted to know,' I said. 'But one last thing Bob, what happens if me and Summer walk down there?'

'You can't Johnny. That's all I want to say.'

'Okay,' I said and walked away. I wondered if they would shoot me in the back.

'That was bad,' Summer said as we drove away. 'We have to be so careful now.'

Back at the station we had to face reality. The smell from Toby's room was rich and pungent. I looked on him again and he seemed to have shifted on his mattress. Toby was face down on the bedding, and appeared to have soiled himself. Who was going to clear up his mess now his wife was dead and burnt I wondered? The carpet was still streaked iron-red with dry blood. I closed the door with a quiet *click*.

'How are the boys doing?' I said to Lester, who was stood at the refreshments room door watching me.

'Good as can be expected I suppose. We just have to look after them the best we can.'

It was Summer who came up with the idea to play football. She saw Phillip and Mark's bleak faces, and told them to find some kit. We crammed into the 4x4 and set off to the local playing field, finding it untended and unloved by any grounds keeper. Weeds were rampant over the patchy grass, and the white frames of the goal posts were more rusted than ever. I suspected we were the first living people to enjoy this place since the outbreak.

'GOAL!' Phillip shouted, as he slotted another one through the bow legs of Lester. Phillip pulled his red football shirt over his head and ran celebrating headlong into his brother. They both fell into a heap laughing and play fighting. Summer and I looked at each other and smiled. Both of us in oversized athletic tops poached out of the lost property bin. She was right as always, this had been the right thing to do. It was helping us all forget where we were for the moment. I looked around us at the empty cricket pavilion and crown green bowling club, left to rot now. Derelict monuments to village times long gone.

'Look,' Summer said. 'He's watching us again.'

I followed her gaze, and there was Griffin swinging on the child's swing. He gave an exaggerated wave our way. It gave me a cold chill.

'What do you think he wants?' she said.

'Just ignore him,' I managed. 'Let's play some more.'

'Okay,' she said. 'But we can't leave Toby for too long. He's going to need us. We're going to have to make him better for the boys.'

I could tell from her face she didn't really believe what she was saying. But she was right, we had to try.

We played the game for another half hour. At some point Griffin must have left. The empty swing seat was rotating gently in the breeze, a forgotten relic once more.

At the station we got the boys to help Lester prepare some food in the kitchen. Summer told them that their Dad was tired, and would see them later. Once they were out of the way it left us with the unfortunate task of cleaning Toby up, and getting some nutrition into him. He was still face down on the mattress, the fever burning up his skin. I went to the window and opened it wider, trying to rid the room of the stench.

'We should burn these,' Summer said, holding up the soiled trousers and underpants. 'Help me with his top.'

'You have a real knack for this,' I said to her, trying hard not to focus on the awful green-black infection spreading beyond the crude arm cast.

'Well, I wasn't always in the police you know. Weekend job at the local old folk's home, The Sanctuary Retreat.'

'I remember now. You told me that just before we went in and cleared the place out. Those zombie grannies were pure evil.'

Summer worked her magic, and in no time Toby was bed bathed and clean. He was stirring now. Not necessarily conscious, but in some netherworld in-between.

'We should have let Lester cut that arm off,' I whispered.

'Maybe.'

'Toby, can you hear me.' I said. 'Come on Toby, we need to eat and drink. You need to get better.'

He twitched and groaned again. I wasn't sure if he was trying to communicate with us.

Summer began to pour a little water in his mouth, but it ran out the sides and pooled on the mattress.

'Tomorrow, we'll ask Lester to sort out a drip. I'm sure he will know how. He'll die quick without water.'

'Maybe ...' Summer started to say, but didn't finish. I knew what she meant.

The mood stayed sombre into the night. It was a blessing that the boys went to sleep fast in Jefferson's old room. They didn't ask too many questions about their Dad. They knew how bad things were. Part of me wondered what kind of parents Summer and I could be to them.

Somewhere after midnight the power went down. One minute we were playing a half-hearted game of poker in the kitchen, and the next we were immersed in black.

I stumbled down to the fuse box, a fire axe in my hand. I half-expected to see the front door swung open and more unwanted guests.

'The door's locked,' I shouted up to Summer.

Nothing in the fuse box was tripped.

Later by the light of the candles we speculated. All the electrics in the station were out, as were the car park street lights.

'It could be the wind turbines again. They were never going to last forever,' Lester said.

'It's the farm,' I said looking into Summer's beautiful flickering face. 'Bob Sack just fucked us over again.'

In the morning I heard engines outside the station. I squinted into the morning light, and I knew what I said had been truth.

Griffin sat out there on a tractor, behind him was a convoy of vehicles. Losing count of the number of guns on display, I ran the windows on the opposite side of the station. The farmers had surrounded us, trapping us. Summer ran into the room, hatchet in her hand. *Always the fearless one.*

'Put it down,' I said. 'We can't win this.'

There was a loud *bang* of someone kicking the front door, and Griffin's booming voice, 'Little pig, little pig ... let me in.'

'Blow his fucking head off,' Lester said walking in.

'We need to play this very cool,' I replied, going for the stairs. 'Stay up here. I think I know what this is about.'

I took in a gulp of air and opened our door.

'Greetings officer,' Griffin said, his father Jack next to him. I counted fifteen others out of their vehicles with

155

guns and assorted weapons. Bob Sack and Jefferson looked prominent in the pack.

'Jack, Griffin. What can I do you for?'

'We've come for a little justice,' Jack said. His nose looked more bulbous and purple than normal, alcohol on his breath.

'Justice is my department. Read the sign. You build fences and fuck sheep, I wear the shiny uniform.'

'No need for profanity, John,' Jack said. I could see Griffin straining at the leash. *Mad dog on heat.*

'What do you expect Jack? Kick on my door, and then stand there like Mad Max and his fucking army. I thought the zombies were all outside the fence now. What's the occasion?'

'The occasion is, Johnny, we want a little word with your new house guest Toby Hanson,' Griffin spat and waved his plastered arm my way. 'What that fucker did to my arm will never be right. Community sentence or some bullshit, well that don't cover this no more.'

'Have you seen Toby recently? After what you did to him, you'll be lucky he lasts the week. Guy's basically in a coma. And while we're on the subject, Jefferson's little zombie took out Mrs Hanson yesterday. Mother of two kids, how you all feeling on that one?' I said raising my voice to a shout. Jefferson looked unmoved, a fully programmed robot.

'You act so whiter than white, don't you Johnny. Where is your good wife these days anyway? We never did work that one out. People we're talking, even before the dead came along. Where did she get to, Johnny?'

'She left Jack, as people are wont to do from time to time,' I looked away, caught out, angry. 'None of your damn business.'

'Anyway, we didn't all come here to talk over the mysteries of your life, Johnny. Save that one for another

156

time. We want Toby Hanson out here in the next five minutes. I don't give a shit about any coma. Just drag whatever is left of that fucker out here, or we'll be going in to get him. And son, that won't be pretty for you or that sweetheart playmate Summer you got in there,' Jack said.

Muscles twitched. I really wanted to cave his face in there and then, starting with that monstrosity of a nose.

'Wait here,' I said at last.

Back inside, my heart was sinking through the floor. Upstairs I faced my friends.

'What was that all about?' Summer said.

'You're going to have to trust me ... a lot!'

A short time later Lester and I were staggering down the stairs with Toby. His eyes flickered, but I don't think he knew what was happening. We zipped a yellow fluorescent police coat over his dirty pyjamas to keep him warm. Toby's pale, gaunt face made him look deader than some of the zombies I'd seen on the streets.

'Is this what you want?' I said to Jack. 'He is all those two boys have left.'

'Take him,' he said to Bob and Griffin.

They dragged Toby over to behind the green farmer's Land Rover. Griffin was hunched over working on something, and then I realised what it was.

'Time to go home,' Jack said smiling.

I felt sick and tried to push Summer and Lester back inside. They were rooted to the spot, like concrete. The Land Rover started with its throaty roar. The other vehicles rumbled away, Griffin and Jack the last to move. There was a dragging sound like sandpaper on rough wood. I saw Toby's body being pulled behind the Land Rover by frayed ropes around his neck and shoulders. His body bounced and the jacket shredded on the grey asphalt. Just as the Land Rover rounded the corner I thought I saw Toby's eyes pop open. A silent scream.

157

'What do we tell the boys?' Summer said to me. Then I heard the crying. They had seen everything.

CHAPTER 27

'So you've decided,' I said, pacing our room.

'We forget the schedule, and we get the hell out of here as soon as possible,' Summer replied. 'We've got extra people now, that's all.'

'The boat will be big enough sure. But are you sure we want to put those kids through more trauma, Summer?'

'We just have to. We stay, we die. It's that simple. Jack and Griffin might have had their blood thirsty fill today, but then there's tomorrow and the day after. I don't want to see you getting dragged behind that Land Rover one day, Johnny.'

'What about these kids?'

'We play the hand we're dealt, Johnny.'

I grabbed my keys. Summer threw coats on Phillip and Mark. They were a pair of ghosts, brains locked down. Orphans now.

'We need your help,' I said crouching to their level. 'We want to sail a boat away from here. Far away from those farmers who hurt your dad. And the zombies ...'

'What the policeman means is we want to take you someplace safe,' Summer finished. 'We all need your help though. Are you okay with that?'

When Phillip and Mark both nodded, she gave them a hug each, maternal instinct kicking in.

'Where's Lester got too?' I asked.

'Down at his lab. You know Lester, always working on something kooky or other,' Summer said.

I wandered through the station and down to the cells. There was mild relief to know he couldn't possibly have another undead subject on his slab, or I'd have known about it. Pushing open the heavy steel cell door, I stepped into Lester's improvised laboratory. The smoky candelabra gave added murk and shadow to the assorted jars, test tubes and cutting implements Lester had collected. The man himself had his head down, one eye peering intently into his secondary school pilfered microscope.

'Lester,' I said. 'We are going to prep and load the boat. Summer thinks we need to step the schedule up. We're looking to go on the high tide tomorrow. Are you okay with that Lester ... Lester? Did you hear anything I just said?'

'I'm on to something here. That swab you gave me. It's a real puzzler, a real conundrum.' Lester said, flicking pages on the textbook next to him. I knew there was no talking to the man in full-blown research mode.

'You got dedication, Lester. We'll talk later, okay?' I said, but he wasn't listening.

Out back I helped cram the last food boxes into the back of the police 4x4. We'd emptied our store cupboard at the station of every tin and packet we had. It wasn't much for five people to live on, but I was sure they'd be more where we were going. I didn't want to risk going back to the shops. Part of me knew Griffin would have already made sure that the aisles would have been stripped bare. Knowing him, he would have probably left a few zombies in there to surprise us. I didn't want to take any more chances.

The drive through the caravan park was quick, but nervy. I half expected to see whatever remained of Bill and Arthur stumbling out in front of us, but the place stayed desolate and empty. The 4x4 sliced through the tangled break in the foliage and out onto the shingle beach. Driving as close to the boat as I dared without risking getting stuck in the sands I parked. The boat WABBA was still there in one piece, held fast by the buoy that had stopped it floating away. The keel was shallow, and I felt sure that we'd be able to sail out in the high tide the next day.

'That's the boat, boys,' I said, hoping for at least a smile. Summer gave them each something light to carry from the back of the 4x4.

'Give them time,' Summer said to me as we walked across the sands.

Jumping aboard, Summer started to find room below for the boxes.

'How's it looking?' I shouted up.

'Like a god-damn miracle is how,' she said. 'You sure you and Lester can sail this thing?'

'Like a dream. Don't you worry about that. My old dad loved his boats, taught me everything he knew.'

The boys finally caught up, and handed up the bits and pieces they had carried over.

'Come on, let's go and get some more,' I said looking at their pale faces. When they didn't move I marched back to the 4x4 alone. I didn't want this to take all day. Throwing a heavy rucksack over my shoulder, I grappled with a box over-flowing with food tins.

'Where are they?' Summer said when as I arrived panting at the boat. And then we saw them, two pinprick figures right out on the sands.

'Jesus, Summer, come on.'

Summer and I ran across the sands. Twenty metres out towards the distant tide line and already the sand was starting to take on the consistency of rice pudding. Shallow seawater puddles squelched and bubbled under our feet, and thin channels of water crisscrossed ahead of us like arterial veins. The boys must have been running as well, trying to cross a bay that drowned, on average, a person a year. Usually it wasn't the quicksand that killed, it was the tide that swept over them while their legs were wrapped in a concrete embrace.

'Johnny look out!' Summer shouted. Too busy looking ahead, I missed what was right under my nose.

Two bodies buried up to their necks. Skin had been peeled from their skulls, the sand and seawater having stripped layers down. Noses, nothing but serrated, fractured bone. Then one opened its mouth, followed by the other. Both still alive like guppies with dagger teeth. I stopped and looked around. There were dozens of similar mounds on the open expanse. Weak zombies trapped and buried by the sands, still looking to bite and tear at anything that passed.

'Phillip! Mark!' I shouted again. 'Come on, the tide will be coming in.'

We ran again, but the boys were so quick. They ran all the way to the tide line. Looking behind me I saw a half mile of flatbed sands stretching back to the shingle beach. The 4x4 looked like a toy car in the distance. We jumped over a small gulley and sprinted the last hundred metres to catch the boys.

'Don't come any closer,' Mark said. 'One of those heads caught my leg.'

His calf muscle had an ugly gash across it, bleeding and smeared in wet sand.

'We need to get you cleaned up,' Summer said, edging nearer. Already Mark's face had taken on that familiar tinge, the bloodless look. He coughed and there was bloody bile on his lips.

'We need to get the both of you back to the beach,' I pleaded. The tide was creeping in, starting to lap around our ankles. The black water scared me. Who knew what it hid?

'Come on, we are running out of time,' I said stepping forward. Phillip had a knife out, waving it towards my chest. The blade nicked my arm. 'What the hell are you doing?'

'You killed everyone, my mum, my dad. They're all dead because of you. You keep away from me and my brother or I'll be killing you.'

162

'Put the knife down Phillip, your brother is sick. He's going to be a zombie, you know that don't you?' I said. 'We need to leave. You know how fast this tide will come in once it's started?'

'We don't leave. We stay right here,' Phillip said. He was cradling his brother's head. It was a matter of time.

'We need to go Johnny,' Summer said. I knew she was right. Already a thin veneer of water was covering half the expanse of sand back to the beach. In a few minutes it would be deep, and we would either drown or get bitten by one of the quicksand zombies.

'Run then.'

And we did. We ran for survival, splashing through to outrun the tide. We just wanted to live. Lying panting on the shingle, I looked out at the sea. There wasn't a single patch of sand to be seen. The sea had smothered everything; it had taken the Hanson boys. I was numb. I wanted to care, but I couldn't quite find the feeling. It was out of reach, walled off by all the death surrounding us.

'We'll be safe on the rig, I know that. We start again,' Summer said.

I followed her gaze; a red light blinking on the horizon. It was all the hope we had left.

CHAPTER 28

Summer threw some water on her face from the small, white sink. She looked at her reflection in the mirror and frowned. Once upon a time, she had spent good money on hairdressers and manicures, now her blonde hair hung in a tangle of tresses. She could pass for a surfer babe maybe, fashionably dishevelled. Summer opened her mouth in an ugly gape, and tried to look at a rear molar. There was an ache there, and she wondered what they would do for dentistry? Perhaps we would all have wooden false teeth, like the middle-ages, she grimaced.

Wandering out of the bathroom, Summer went down the corridor to Lester's smoke-choked little den.

'Are you sure about any of this?' she heard Johnny say.

'I've seen it with my own eyes,' Lester insisted. 'The alien thing in the blood, the virus that started this nightmare, is man-made. I don't know that much about the science, but I know nature doesn't make things that perfect. I believe what I am seeing through the microscope is a synthetic artefact. I have read scientists in America have been able to create a living poliovirus, that there was a recipe downloadable on the internet. The journals say it is a simple virus to make. They talked of smallpox being the next step. I think somebody made this thing.'

'Is this a government conspiracy theory, Lester?' Summer said. 'Have you been back on the booze? How can you tell anything through that old microscope?'

'Well, okay I can't see things on a genetic level,' Lester went on. 'It's instinct partly. The way it's acting. It's a blood borne virus that can take effect in minutes. There's nothing in nature that can work that fast, nothing that does what this does. Even the smallest exposure appears deadly.'

'Apart from you, Lester, you're immune remember,' Summer reminded him. 'Although for my money that might be wishful thinking.'

'Okay, Lester, say you're right,' said Johnny. 'What if it wasn't the government? I mean they seem as dead as everyone else. There's been no helicopters or planes in the sky, or even radio messages. There's no evidence to show politicians or military survived, or have any power still. They appear to have been caught unawares just like the rest of us. What if it was somebody else who did this?'

'Bio-terrorism?' Lester added. 'Took the words right out of my mouth.'

'And you know what that means? We should watch our backs, that's what. If your kooky theory is right, the next batch of survivors to jump the fence could well be the damn people behind it all,' Summer said.

'Oh course, it's just a theory. Got no way to test in reality, not with just this old microscope anyway,' Lester said patting the black, metal contraption on his desk.

'Maybe one day, Lester. Priority now is to get the hell out of here with the skin still on our backs,' Johnny said.

'So we make for the rig at first light tomorrow, when the tide is up,' Lester said. 'Makes sense. Those farmers are all damned psychos these days.'

'Agreed,' Johnny said. Summer liked it when he did his tough man act.

'Let's go and grab some lunch. Not much left now that isn't already packed on the boat. Hope you like rice cakes,' Summer smiled.

Later, she shared a cigarette with Johnny in the car park. The old orders read no smoking on police premises. It seemed old habits died hard, as they always came outside here to smoke. She felt the questions still nagging at her.

'Do you miss her, Johnny?'

'My wife? I told you, we were estranged, Summer. She went down to London, some younger lover. I've told you that before.'

'Do you not wonder what happened to her? She might have survived you know. Have you thought of going to look?'

'Can't say I have. She's gone, Summer. She didn't love me, and the feeling was mutual. Drop it will you.'

'You are always so touchy, makes me think there was something you're not telling me ... Forget about it, I'm being stupid. Just a bit emotional after the boys went,' she said at last, and hugged him. Johnny was her man. She would die for him, she was pretty sure. 'When we sit here sometimes I can make myself forget everything that's happened. It just seems like another normal day. You know, go to a few community meetings, go home and drink a good bottle of red wine and watch a DVD.'

'Hope I factor into this scenario, honey,' Johnny said smiling. 'I like wine and DVD's too, you know. Any chance of an invite?'

'No, no gatecrashers allowed in my daydreams,' she said and tickled his ribs.

'Let's go for a walk Johnny. Watch the sunset over this village one last time.'

Summer chose the route, and guided them through a cut-through that led down to a causeway above the beach. To their left was an expansive lawn of a country house, long split into apartments. The grass looked heavy with dead wood and leaves, no grounds keeper to keep it clean. They watched grey squirrels roll and gather chestnuts among the sticks. Carefree and abundant in numbers, they looked happy with their new world.

'How would you catch a squirrel?' Johnny said.

'Don't even think it.'

They walked on to the old boathouse, derelict years before the outbreak came. It was once a place where yachts were brought out of the water for servicing. Now it was just an empty husk of a warehouse on the beachfront. Smashed windows and a rusting metal corrugated roof.

'Let's go off the beaten track,' Summer said, steering them on to a rubble, uphill path.

'We're not going to see many sunsets up here,' Johnny said.

'Changed my mind. My prerogative you know.'

The path took them up steeply. They passed a small shack that once sold ice cream, the gloomy windows broken and the green paint peeled off the doorframes. Like the boat yard, it had been derelict for years. The path took them higher and into the canopy of woods. They both started to breathe a little heavier, not used to exercise after months of cautious movements.

'We turn off here,' Summer pointed. 'I used to climb this easy.'

'So you've been here before? When you were at work?'

'No, when I was a kid, silly. Me and my friends used to come here a lot. To drink and smoke. Come on, I'll show you.'

Summer pushed the dense foliage out of the way and stepped off the path. She half-remembered the way through the oaks and willows, and was pleased to find the faint trodden trail still in the soil.

'This way, Johnny,' she said. To her right she saw a high stone wall, with what looked like a small castle rising above it. She remembered climbing it once in her youth, and finding the exciting castle was actually no more than somebody's garden shed, filled with boring gardening tools. Summer followed the line of the wall and went deeper into the trees. Through the leaves and branches they could just make out the roof of the manor house apartments they had seen from the beach.

'So what was this place?' Johnny said touching a blue rope net attached to a tree. It tore in his hand when he pulled at it, rotten.

'This place used to be an adventure playground believe it or not,' Summer said, walking up to an old tyre swing. The rubber was green with mould, and the rope just a few thin threads. 'No swinging today I guess. Back in the day, the old house at the bottom was outward bound for under-privileged kids. Went bust, and for a time it was an adventure playground for us village kids.'

'So this place was your mis-spent youth.'

'Yeah, kind of. Drinking and carousing, you name it.'

'So, did you bring boys down here, for a good time?'

'Jeez, Johnny Silverman. Are you jealous?'

'Yeah well, that's my prerogative, okay,' Johnny said smiling. 'Seriously, your whoring is of no interest to me really.'

That earned him a punch on the arm. They sat for a while, catching the sunset through the trees, the orange ball sliding down behind the hills that lined the far side of the bay. Summer felt the warm tingle of happiness that could only be love. She had found her soulmate finally at the end of the world.

They retraced their steps before it got too dark. Summer was starting to hear things rustling further into the woods, and she wanted to go back on to the beach.

'It's just deer, I'm sure,' Johnny said.

Sliding and walking down the steep incline of the path, Summer thought she saw something move. 'Did you see that?' she said, pointing at a distant garden.

'See what?'

'I thought I saw somebody crouch down quick. A body maybe?'

168

'Wait here,' Johnny said and walked up the garden path to the house next to the ice cream hut.

There was a garden feature, a wishing well she guessed, big enough for a person to hide behind. 'Be careful,' she shouted. Her heart was in her mouth as she watched Johnny get closer. For a second it looked like there was nothing there, then Johnny stepped back, rigid, scared of something, she thought. Maybe there was a body after all? A man stood up from behind the well, the bulky, round-faced man from the farm. Bob Sack had a gun in his hand.

'Run,' Johnny shouted, but was cut off when the fat man hit him on the side of the head. Johnny collapsed, and Sack looked her dead in the eyes. Instinct took over. Summer turned and ran for the beach. Rounding the corner onto the causeway, she saw more figures coming towards her. Turning round, Summer jumped down to the beach, sprinting. Above, a figure emerged from the ruin of the boat yard.

'You can run if you like, Summer,' Jefferson said. 'Won't do you no good though.'

CHAPTER 29

Tied like a hog, Summer bounced on the metal floor of the transit van. The binds locking her wrists behind her back dug in, painfully cutting off the circulation to her hands. The fat man Sack sat to one side of her, still rubbing his cheek where she'd raked her fingernails down. A small revenge for what he'd done to Johnny. Was he still alive? She wondered. The men had chased her down the beach and tackled her onto the sand. Summer had fought like a wild animal until Jefferson had hit her. Not a slap, but a full-blooded punch that had loosed two of her teeth and sent her down in a dazed heap.

'You know where you're going don't you, Summer,' Jefferson sneered from the driver's seat. 'The farm is where you belong now. No call for police anymore. We police our own way.'

'I hope the government roll up tomorrow. I'd love to see you hung from the nearest tree, you fucking psychopath.'

'Anyone gets hung around here, it's you and your boyfriend. I'd be on your best behaviour if I was you,' Bob Sack carped back.

That was all the information she wanted. Johnny must still be alive. If he wasn't in this van he might be in the van behind. If not there, then he had been left nursing a head injury. She swore if Johnny died Bob Sack would pay a heavy price. Summer tried to relax and take some of the pain out of her wrists as they trundled out of the village.

'Last stop,' shouted Bob Sack, and the double doors at the back of the van flew open. She felt calloused hands on her arms pulling her out. For a split second, the sunlight hurt her eyes, and then her senses clicked in all at once. The stench and the mess, the place she hated more than anywhere left in the world. She wanted to see this farm burn one day.

'Let me show you to your quarters,' Griffin said appearing at the van's back doors. 'Not the most luxurious, but it will have to do. Until you are more ... domesticated.'

Summer was on her feet now, and Griffin had one hand tight on the crook of her elbow. She felt helpless with her hands still behind her back. 'So did you bring me her boyfriend as well, that gutless cop Silverman?'

'He got a clout, could be dead. We just brought the girl,' Bob Sack said.

'You are a sack of shit, Sack,' Griffin replied.

'Griffin, these binds are too tight. They're cutting off the circulation to my hands. You're going to have to take them off,' Summer said as Griffin pushed her not towards the farmhouse, but the decrepit old barn off to one side.

'Let's see if you want to behave first. Might just let those pretty hands go black and fall off. How would you like that?'

Summer watched Griffin bring a key up to the heavy padlock and click it open. She took one last look back at the farm courtyard. So, Johnny was still out there somewhere, she thought, deciding she wouldn't bring him up in conversation. Act like she didn't care as much as she did. Summer saw all the villagers running around doing their farm chores. All drones now, worker ants without an independent thought in their heads. They were the real zombies.

The barn door opened, and the dank, rotten smell hit her. 'You can't be serious,' she said.

'Not the Ritz, but it doesn't have to always be like this,' Griffin said marching her inside. 'Show me you can behave and we'll see about moving you into the big house.'

Summer looked around. The barn had a series of wooden stalls, like horses stables. Dull light filtered down from the breaks in the roof. The ground was a mixture of hard packed soil and broken wooden boards. The place creaked and groaned like it was alive itself.

'What's with all these tents, Griffin? What are you trying to hide under them?' Summer said. She was sure she heard movement. Distracted, she didn't even notice Griffin snapping the iron bracelet on her ankle. Five feet of chain lead to a metal supporting pillar. Griffin cut her binds off, her hands completely numb.

'Can't have you running away, can we?' Griffin said. 'And as for what's under the sheets, well let's take a look.'

Griffin walked along the stalls pulling the tarpaulins away. The zombies beneath stirred from their stupor. Summer counted five women strapped and nailed to wooded boards, almost as if they had been crucified, some upright, others horizontal. All naked, all mutilated in some way or other. At least two had their breasts cut away, leaving bloodied open wounds.

'You are sick, Griffin!' Summer shouted.

'Not so loud, you'll offend my brother,' he said pulling off the final sheet. There was what was left of a young man, green-black with the rot in his limbs. The skin in his face had mostly gone. All that seemed left was an ugly grin of teeth, and dry sunken eyes that seemed somehow lost. 'My younger brother, Dexter. Got to look after family, don't we? He was always the sensitive one.'

'I wonder what the villagers would make of all this sickness,' Summer said.

'I do what I want, Summer,' Griffin said and walked away. 'I'll be back later. Might even feed you if you play your cards right.'

She watched him leave and heard the padlock locked back on. She turned back towards the bodies. Every one of them straining to get to her. If even one of them broke free, she would be torn to pieces. She tried not to make eye contact.

An hour went by. Summer heard muffled voices from time to time, and the sounds of construction nearby. Eventually she had enough of standing and moved to sit down and lean against the side of the barn. She figured she might be able to kick the boards out of the wall, but that would still leave her attached to the chain. Summer scrabbled around the earth looking for an implement to work on the padlocked manacle around her ankle. All the time the bodies thrashed and moaned, and she tried to ignore them. Eventually, she gave it up and lay down. There was no way out.

Summer thought about her family. She hated remembering. Every time the black void of depression and despair would open up to claim her whole. Random Christmas memories, the sense of family togetherness and presents, she couldn't stop them flooding her mind. It hurt that those times would never be repeated, not after hacking whatever life remained out of her mother and father. It made her feel unclean and dirty. Is this how murderers feel, she wondered? All she had now was Johnny. She wanted to believe he was still alive and coming to save her. If he was dead she would make these people pay a dear price for their sadism.

'Are you asleep?' she heard a woman's voice say. Summer's eyes came back into focus. It was darker now inside the barn. She felt a terrible crick in her neck from sleeping on the cold ground.

'Who are you?'

'Alison, Jack's partner. I came to bring you something to eat,' the plump woman said. 'I told Griffin he shouldn't do this, that you should be in the house. But he won't listen to me tonight. A stubborn man.'

173

'Have you got the key, Alison? You know they have kidnapped me. Attacked the policeman and hurt him.'

'I just came to bring you this,' Alison said laying down some steaming stew to the side.

Summer instinctively reacted and grabbed at Alison's jumper tripping her off-balance. She rolled herself on top of Alison and pinned her arms back on the earth. 'Where is that fucking ankle key bitch?'

'Get off me, you're hurting.'

'I'll hurt you a hell of a lot more if you don't produce that key to unlock me. Now which pocket?' Summer hissed, driving one of her knees into the side of Alison's ribs.

'Griffin has it. He's got the only one.'

'Show me.'

Summer watched as Alison reached into her trouser pocket and rooted out a solitary key. Summer took it and ran her hands over the pockets to make sure there wasn't another one hiding. Pulling away slightly from Alison she tried the key in the lock of the bracelet. It didn't even fit half-way in. Summer stood up and walked a chain's length away in disgust.

'I need to get the hell away from here,' she said at last.

'You need to survive, we all do,' Alison said brushing the dirt off her clothes. 'Help me get clean, or they won't trust me enough to let me in here again. It could be bad for you too.'

Summer did as she was asked. 'So how did you end up with Jack? Johnny told me you were new here at the farm, that you weren't here before the outbreak.'

'I wasn't, I was walking with my husband at the tower when those things came and took him from me. Griffin found me cowering at the top, half-dead from the cold. They took me in and Jack took a shine to me. As long as I do what I'm told, I survive. I don't always like it but

174

what can I do? I don't want to die. I don't want to end up one of those monsters.'

'I guess kidnap and murder are just par for the course these days, hey?' Summer said.

'I can't change the way things are these days. I know it's wrong, but I have to live here too. I have to live with Jack and Griffin however misguided they get. Look, I have to get back; they'll be wondering why I took so long. I'll make sure you get breakfast. Just try and rest some more.'

'Look at these things here Alison. Don't you know what Griffin does with them?' Summer spat.

'I don't want to know,' Alison said and walked out of the barn.

Restless and frustrated she knelt down and ate the stew Alison had brought. It was the first food she hadn't eaten out of a tin or a foil packet in months, and it tasted delicious. Whatever that woman had degraded into, she could certainly cook a good meal, Summer thought. Finally, the last of the light through the gaps in the roof faded and she was left with the darkness. The constant shifting and rustling of the tethered dead unnerved her. The smell didn't go away either. The rot in the air was tangible, almost as if she could taste the dead skin cells in the air. She lay down again and shivered. It would be a long, cold night.

Woken, there were twin bulbs of light blinding and burning her retinas. Low rumbling voices. She blinked and rubbed at her eyes.

'Can't you people just leave me alone!' she shouted. The torches waved in the air, as if floating. She caught a flash of pink skin, a distended belly like a hairy brown boulder.

'Who are you?' she shouted into the darkness.

'Don't you recognise us without our clothes?' A deep growl. Not Griffin, older.

175

'My Da always goes first,' another voice said. Now Summer knew, and she screamed.

CHAPTER 30

My head felt like something was trying to drill its way out. I'd thought the phrase *seeing stars* was just a saying, but the haze of rainbow colours dancing in my peripheral vision told me different. Bob Sack had knocked me cold. I kicked myself for not seeing it coming, basically for not ducking. Picking myself up off the dirt path, my fingers went to touch around the pain area. There was an Emu sized egg growing out the back of my skull. Touching tentatively around the edges, I felt the dry, clotted blood, lots of it. Dizzy, I retched, a watery mix on my trouser leg and shoes. How long I had been unconscious? The moonlit sky gave no clue.

Wobbling back down the path to the causeway path like a 3am drunk, there was no sign of Summer or Bob Sack or anybody else. Nothing there but squawking white gulls on the shoreline, picking the meat off another dead dog. Dead pets were common in the village. No room for sentiment.

The walk back to the station was a long one. More often than not I found myself bent over, dry heaving what was left of my stomach contents. It was likely concussion. My police Freelander had been defiled, tyres gouged and unintelligible graffiti etched onto the liveried paintwork. I walked round it and punched in the door code for the station's front door. If anybody waited for me inside I knew I was in no condition to fight, but blundered in anyway.

'Lester, are you in here? I shouted into the dark. 'LESTER!'

In the downstairs hallway, I caught a glimpse of a shadow moving in the photocopying room. I charged it, pure bubbling rage that suddenly needed an outlet. The shadow could have been a body or somebody with a gun. This would be how I would go out.

'What the fuck are you doing hiding in here?' I ranted, shaking the man like a rag doll.

'Take those big paws of me for a second and I'll tell ya,' Lester said. 'God-damn scared me half to death.'

We lit a candle and I told him what had happened to Summer and me. He was halfway sympathetic when I showed him the state of the back of my head.

'They came here for me too, kicked the back door clean off its hinges. I was a step ahead though, heard those diesels coming a mile off. They never thought to look in the loft, stupid idiots. They stole quite a few bits, weapons and the like. Don't think we've got much to fight those sheep shaggers with now 'cept the skin off our knuckles.'

'They got it coming now Lester. I'm going straight there and I'm going to get her back,' I said.

'You do that son, and I might as well stoke a fire up in the back car park right now. A frontal assault isn't going to do anything other than get you killed before you even set eyes on Summer. Shouldn't take an old vagrant like me to tell a smart officer like yourself this will need some brain work.'

'Alright, Lester, we do it smart.'

'And speaking of smart, they might have realised by now it wasn't very intelligent to leave you still sucking on air. Could be they're going to come back looking for an easy kill. Much as we love this place, we need to haul somewhere unexpected like. Any ideas?'

'Yeah I got one,' I answered.

I kicked at the door, and then brought my shoulder hard against the wood. It bulged but didn't give.

'Try these,' Lester shrugged, waving a set of keys in front of my nose. 'Plant pot.'

'Why didn't you say?' I said and snatched them out of his hand. My idea for somewhere safe was the village train station. It wasn't directly on the road, and only accessible by walking down a hundred metres of track from the train station. With no buildings or trees close for cover, we'd be able to see anybody approaching, and hopefully be ready for them. As all the trains were long gone, this was probably one of the last places the farmers would think to look for us.

Inside the room was an array of antiquated levers and switches that controlled the track and the signals. The body of the signalman was lying on the floor, still in his starchy tweed uniform. He looked like he'd gone through the change at some point, the rictus anger still visible in his face. When a zombie died, they kept that evil biting look.

We'd been lucky though, as it appeared the undead signalman had cracked open his skull on one of the heavy metal levers that dominated the room.

'So you ever been down there before,' Lester said pointing at the door to downstairs.

'No, but I'm pretty sure there will be living quarters. The council kept the signal box for heritage reasons. This guy here was a widower I believe, John or James; I forget. I used to see the lights on late doing my patrol, long after the last trains had gone. I'm pretty sure he must have lived here too.'

'Best make sure we black out those windows, or we'll end up with company,' Lester said, going down.

We were short on weapons now the farmers had cleared us out. Lester had a heavy wooden club and I had dug out an old rusted machete from the ransacked weapons store at the police station. Pitch black in the bedsit style apartment below, I washed the light from my torch around the kitchen diner, and then over into the single bedroom. There was nobody else home. The decor reminded me of the late 1950's, nasty brown wallpaper and framed pictures of steam engines. There were pictures of the village eighty or a hundred years earlier. Pictures of everyday people long since turned to dust. The place was a wreck, broken crockery strewn all over the cramped lounge kitchen. It occurred to me that the change had taken the signalman down here, perhaps after staggering back, bitten by a passing commuter.

'This will do in the short-term,' I said. 'We just take turns on the look out, and keep the lights down or out at night. I don't plan on being here long.'

I didn't have a watch but I estimated it was around four hours to dawn. The plan was to take hourly turns on lookout, but in the end, neither of us could sleep. We both found ourselves staring out of the small window in the bedroom. It gave a reasonable view of the road below the seven foot drop on the other side of the track and railway fencing. It was an hour before we saw movement, a farm truck moving slowly past. We saw it three more times as it circled the village.

'Looking for us, no doubt,' I said.

'It was that fuck Jefferson driving as well. Never trusted that man. Deserves all he has coming,' Lester snorted.

'We need to take our time with this thing, don't we? Or we all die.'

At first light we moved. I picked the most obscure footpaths that led from the village into the woods. It took an hour, but eventually we fought our way through the trees and brambles to get close to the farm check-point without being seen. Lester raised an antique pair of binoculars to his eyes. 'Amazing what one can find,' he said.

It looked like they had beefed up security. I counted six armed men at the entrance to the farm track. In the distance there were figures walking the fields and around the tower. 'Armed too. And can't see Summer anywhere,' Lester confirmed. The farmhouse was guarded from every side.

'How are we going to do this thing, Lester?'

'Carefully, and not today,' he answered. 'I got some ideas, don't you worry about that. We'll get her back alright.'

Picking our way to the signal box, we made the last leg over the railway footbridge a mad dash. To be spotted now would be a disaster. I felt sure that if Jack or Griffin got their hands on me then what happened to Toby would be nothing. Sinking back into the gloom of the living quarters I paced nervously up and down in the cramped room, smashed plates crunching under my feet. Lester lit a candle.

'Too many guns Lester, they'll cut us down before we even step foot in that farmyard. God knows what they're doing to Summer down there,' I said, hacking a blunt tin opener into a beans can I'd found in the cupboard.

'You forget old Lester is germinating a plan up here,' Lester said tapping a finger on his temple.

We ate, and still Lester wasn't for sharing his plan. Over the months, I'd got used to his idiosyncratic ways. I trusted the guy now, whereas back in the day all I'd seen him as was a nuisance, or an easy arrest for drunk and disorderly. Times had changed, and he had too. He'd turned into the brains of this operation.

'We need a canoe,' Lester said at last. 'And some damn fine luck.'

When the sun went down, we were back outside. 'I know a place from when I was scavenging. There's a nice old Canadian canoe waiting for us. Beach house, not far from the water,' Lester said.

'What the hell are you thinking exactly?' I said. He had to tell me twice before I believed him.

Fifteen minutes of creeping through the shadows and we got the house. An odd-looking place, that looked

181

like it sat on stilts under a triangular roof. Trust Lester to take us to the strangest house in the village. It must have attracted him like a magnet. The garage door lifted up a terrible shriek of scratching metal. I looked around terrified that somebody had heard us. There was nothing there but the outline of swaying trees and the rush of water from the incoming tide.

'Christ this is heavy, Lester,' I said, as we heaved the Canadian canoe out of the garage. We put it down on the driveway and went back for the paddles.

'Leave the life jackets, they're all too bright. Last thing we want to do is stick out like a sore thumb on the water. Hope you can swim okay, Lester.'

'Like a fish.'

The canoe was an old wooden thing, and must have weighed sixty kilos easy. As we dragged it into the rising water I thought of Mark and Phillip, and all the dead heads sunk in the sand. The freezing water was up to my knees before the thing floated enough for us to get in. The chill on the air didn't help, and I wished I'd worn more clothes. The moon seemed horribly bright, making me feel very exposed out on the water. The tide dragged us towards the silhouetted railway bridge in the distance. Lester sat in the back digging his paddle in, trying to steer.

'Paddling back will be a bitch,' I said, trying to make a joke as the bridge loomed up ahead. Suddenly it was clear just how fast we were travelling, and how big the buttresses on the bridge appeared.

'Steer for the middle,' I shouted. I could see we were heading straight for one of the stone supports. I could hear the tearing power of the water against the stone, and see the channels turning into torrents. If we capsized, the undertows would drag us down. Our bodies would be broken on the rocks below.

I dug my oar in hard with Lester's and tried to turn us. The current had us and the canoe slammed against a buttress sending wood chip splinters exploding into my face. We rocked and spun out of control, as the hard spray from the cauldron of water hit repeatedly. My paddle tore out of my grasp, and I readied myself to be flung to the depths. Then all at once, we were out of the vortex and on other side of the bridge, colliding with something in the water with a dull *thud*. I looked down and saw a reaching body in the water.

'FUCKING PADDLE LESTER!'

The push of the tide eased the further we went down the bay, and we took turns with the one paddle we had left. We travelled the two miles we needed in little over an hour. It was perhaps the most scared I had ever been. I squinted in the moonlight and tried to navigate around the bodies we kept seeing. The walking dead caught out by the tide. They bobbed and floated. Sometimes we felt a scrape on the bottom of the canoe. I wanted to think it was just deadwood or a sand bank, but in my mind, I knew it was more bodies. They didn't all float, some were sinkers, reaching out for us through the black water. We were far beyond the safety of the fence line now; we were deep in *their* territory.

'We head for that peninsula,' Lester said pointing.

From pulling ashore, it was a straight scared-to-death run off the beach. I rushed climbing a wooden stile and fell flat on my face onto the sand at the other side. My palms burned where I grazed them. I looked up to see the unmistakeable gait of a body above me, then it fell as well.

'Come on, we have to move,' Lester whispered, the short lead pipe in his hand clumped with brain.

We crossed the main road in a hurry, and found the track. The ground was uneven and covered with potholes and puddles. The smell of rotting flesh hung in the air. We were deep in the dead zone.

'This is it,' Lester said, panting and coughing up phlegm. I pulled the torch out of the pocket and switched it on. Lester looked in bad shape; we were both exhausted. The sign he was leaning on read, 'BEWARE: HEAVY QUARRY TRAFFIC.'

We climbed the padlocked gate and started up the dirt road into the quarry. Ahead the outlines of great excavators lay dormant and quiet. I felt for a second like we'd stumbled into the land of the giants. Lester seemed to know where he was going; I followed a pace behind.

'You going to be able to run if you have to?' I asked him.

'Fight or flight my friend.'

Lester went to a portacabin that sat next to the main entrance to the quarry warehouse. 'Wait,' I said, too full of myself. I twisted the corroded handle open and stepped up. The smell brought back memories of the shot foot and mouth cattle, left too many days in the baking sun waiting to be incinerated. The bulbous body lurched out of the shadows and caught my clothing, his mass sending me careering backward into a filing cabinet. Something sharp dug in and cut open my shin. I wanted it not to be teeth.

'Lester! Get in here!'

I felt myself pushed slowly off-balance and down. His weight was smothering, and it was taking all my strength to stop that awful mouth from clamping down and ending me. A dull *clunk-crack* and the fat man's head was a broken water melon. Lester's lead pipe was buried in deep, sticking out of the fat man's cranium like busted drainpipe. He didn't drop though, and turned on Lester. The teeth had a finger off, then two. Lester screamed, and I staggered to my feet. The pipe was in my hands, and I drove it deeper into

184

the brain, pulling and stirring at it as if it was thick porridge. The body dropped at last, Lester's howls filling the silence.

'We need to stop the blood,' I said tearing a strip off my own trousers.

'Jesus Johnny, two fingers gone in the fat man's mouth. It hurts like a mother fucker.'

I wrapped the improvised bandage tight around the exposed bones and torn skin. Lester's blood covered me before I even thought about infection. I wondered how quick the change would come for him, and how I was ever going to rescue Summer alone?

'I found the keys,' I told Lester. 'They were in fat man's desk.'

Outside I expected more company, but the quarry was still as desolate as before. We crunched our way further into the quarry. To our left the rock face was in view; two hundred foot of limestone cliff.

'Have you been here before, Lester?'

'Used to work here believe it or not. Fired me for drinking on the job,' he said through gritted teeth.

Finally, there was a steel container half the size of the portacabin, surrounded by wire fencing. Lester had been right when he'd told me we'd never break in, The place looked like a miniature Fort Knox. Heavy bolts on the outer gate gleaming new steel. Above our heads was a set of CCTV cameras on a high pole. We moved through the gate and I wrenched open the heavy doors in the container.

'How are you feeling?' I asked, and flicked the torch onto Lester's face. I expected to see signs the virus was taking hold. There were none. Lester was unchanged.

'Damn it Lester, you are immune!'

'Beats winning the lottery any day,' he smiled. 'Not my fault you never believed me. Now help me with this box here. Careful like.'

We lifted it outside, deceptively heavy for its size. Lester peeled off the tape and opened the lid. Thirty grey sticks like candles, each capable of blowing the limbs from your body.

'We're in business now, ain't we,' Lester grinned.

CHAPTER 31

Jack Nation looked out of his bedroom window. There wasn't much to see other than spot lights set up at the far end of the farm track. He could just make out the figures sitting around at the check-point. The night shift. Smokers and chin scratchers to a man. There would be words in the morning. Further right still was the faint silhouette of the fence. His master work, his legacy to the world. Sometimes after too many malts, he wondered what his Daddy would have made of it all? Would he think he was a good man, helping all these people?

A step back and he was looking at his craggy reflection, the bulbous, veined nose that wouldn't stop growing out. They had dragged what was left of Toby Hanson all the way home. Nothing left in the end but a bloody streak of meat. He thought of what they'd done to Summer as well ...

'Jack, are you coming back to bed?' Alison's nagging voice.

'Right you are.'

Out of the corner of his eye something moved, drawing him back to the window. A light crossing the window, it was bright like a shooting star. The men's shouts carried all the way from the check-point. Something was coming towards them, something on fire! In the orange flames, he could just make out the shape of a car as it hit the horse wagon and burst into a mushroom of fire, an explosion that lifted the men and scattered them about like dandelion seeds on the wind. Jack pulled away, grabbed his clothes in rough handfuls.

'Stay put, you hear?' he said.

'Dad, what we do?' Griffin shouted, bursting into the room. He face was ash-white.

'Get the men, all you can find. Guns, lots of them.'

A second explosion, closer, making the windows shudder in their frames. Sound hitting like thunder. Jack ran back to the window and saw dirty flames lighting up a section of his fence. The hush of dead shapes pouring onto his land.

'They're coming, Griffin! Get everyone in the yard. Send them out, send them now!'

Jack threw on the rest of his clothes and grabbed his shotgun. He emptied two boxes of shells on to the dresser, spilling half on the floor. Jack's hands were shaking.

'What about me?' he heard Alison say from the bed.

Ignoring her, he went out into the corridor. Half-dressed, half-asleep men and woman were coming out of their rooms, all full of questions. Jack pushed some, threw others towards the stairs. 'Get out there and fight. Fight or die,' he told everyone he saw.

The sharp blast and pop of gunfire already reverberated from the farmyard. Jack slipped into one of the vacated bedrooms to watch, unwilling to risk everything yet. Waves of putrid dead were flowing into the yard under a white blaze halogen lights. Two lines of the men, perhaps thirty in number, were cutting loose with their firearms. Jack drilled them for this day; he knew they were ready. The front dead fell, but others filled their place. The Land Rover petrol diesel tank exploded, lighting up the fields beyond. There was an endless queue of dead, all waiting patiently for their turn. There could have been a thousand, there could have been more.

'Zulu,' muttered out of Jack's lips.

'I seen 'em,' Griffin said, rushing in.

Jack turned on his son. 'I see 'em too. Hard to miss, son.'

'Not them, not the bodies, the live ones who did this. I seen 'em sneaking around the back,' Griffin pointed at the side of the old barn.

And there they were, clear as day. Officer Johnny and the vagrant, Lester, crowbarring the lock off the barn door. Jack looked from them back to the men at the front of the farmhouse, already scattered and disorganised. Half had fallen and were being devoured, their carcasses lost in the sheer numbers of the bodies. He counted at least five of his men dead and risen up against him. One still swung a gun, caught in the claw of his hand.

'Get Jefferson and Sack,' Jack barked. 'We go out the fire-escape. We finish the fucking copper this time.'

CHAPTER 32

'We're in,' I shouted across to Lester, a hard thing to do in the white noise of the war raging around us. It was like having your head inside a raging waterfall. I swung the barn door open and we ran inside. Both us were still panting from racing the dead to the farm. After we had fired the detonators, we'd been caught by surprise, never expecting the dead to come through so fast. All that pressure pushing on the fence had suddenly released, almost like champagne overflowing the neck of a bottle.

'Summer!' I shouted and Lester joined me. I pulled back plastic sheeting horrified at what I might find. I was horrified anyway, and thanked God she wasn't there.

'Lester, have some seen this?' Stall upon stall of twisted sexual fantasy. Undead, naked woman bound down and writhing. Tearing up the flesh around straps binding their limbs, each one of them muzzled not to bite.

'Sick minds in this playground.'

'Griffin, no doubt. The boy ain't right,' Lester said.

'Summer!' I shouted again. My dragon light battery was low, the weak beam barely reaching the dark corners of the barn. The gunshots outside were more sporadic, one side was winning the war. The dead were beginning to grind against the side of the barn. They sensed us, I was sure.

'We don't have time, Lester, we need to find her now,' I said. Behind me I heard the barn door slam shut. I turned, expecting dead faces, but out of the shadows came Jack and Griffin, then Bob Sack and the traitor Jefferson.

'Quite a party you started,' Jack said, flashing his own torch. The others aimed shotguns at my chest. I wondered how much it was going to hurt. 'Throw the weapons down, if you can call them that.'

I tossed my lead pipe to the dirt floor. Lester's machete followed it.

'Won't be needing these anymore,' Griffin sneered, as he collected them. He stepped forward and pulled us both down. The wide barrels dissuaded me from making any kind of move.

'What have you done with Summer?' I asked, my throat dry.

'It was a romantic gesture, I give you that. Destroying my fence, my farm, my people, for just a woman,' Jack said. 'And don't worry, you'll be getting the proper reward.'

'My reward will be cutting your gutless heart out,' Griffin added, showing his black teeth.

'I'm sure you can patch a fence up, Jack; might even keep you out of trouble for a few weeks. You know, once upon a time, people that shagged corpses went to the prison with the padded cells. Maybe you could build one of those next,' I said. Griffin looked down for an instant. Bob and Jefferson appeared curious about the stalls. I had a feeling this was the first time they'd seen what Griffin did in his spare time. 'Sick new world, isn't it, gents?'

'It's for my brother, Dexter, really; a little company. Maybe I play a little too, it's a free country,' Griffin said, red tinges on his cheeks.

'Look,' I said, 'whatever you do with me, just leave Lester out of it. He's a good, clever man and you will need him around here. He was just helping me because he felt he owed me.'

'No need to worry, son,' Lester said, low and careful to me. 'I made my peace.'

The clattering of dead against the walls of the barn was getting louder. I saw grey, dead hands reaching in through gaps in the wooden planks. 'We need to make a move,' Jack said. The bound zombies thrashed at their binds, sensing their brethren were close by. Suddenly Dexter was loose, his rotten ties snapping and trailing behind. The mouth still gagged, Griffin ran forward and tackled him to the floor. I darted left and a shot rang out. I heard Lester cry out and saw him bleeding on the floor, his stomach strafed with shotgun pellets.

'You're next, Johnny,' I heard Jack shout, Griffin swinging his shotgun stock towards my face. Too quick to duck, it hit me and the world went black.

'Finish him now,' I heard Griffin screech, the words distorting in my swimming head.

'No,' Jack's voice said. 'We want to do him slow.'

Bob Sack's fat hands were dragging me to the door, the cold wind on my face, as it suddenly swung open. Jack and Griffin started firing repeatedly. Heads exploded like over-ripe pumpkins. Splattering gore hit my face like rain. My legs were rubber and I had no strength to break away.

'We can't make the farmhouse,' Jack shouted. 'We go to the new build and lock in.'

More bodies fell with shots and clubbing blows. The half-finished breeze-block building loomed up as I fought to raise my head and not black out. Bob Sack threw me roughly through the entrance, and a heavy door slammed shut.

'Thank God we made this door. Fucker's won't get through this in a hurry,' Griffin's voice came out of the dark. From outside I heard many hands pounding on the metal. Touches were switched on and I realised that Lester wasn't with us. Shot and left like a piece of meat in the barn, the thought made me sick with anger. It looked like Jefferson hadn't made it inside either, lost in the melee.

'Summer!' I shouted. I wanted her still to be alive, the loneliness and grief tangible.

'She's upstairs, you'll see her before you leave tonight,' Jack whispered.

The half-finished entrance hall smelt of plaster dust. Torch beams danced on the white walls and stairs as I was hustled upward. Bare wires and cables hung down unfinished, and I brushed them away from my faces as we climbed. Tools were everywhere, and I found myself looking for a useful weapon. Jack and Griffin were trailing behind me with their guns. At least I would go down fighting, not tortured in some sick fantasy.

'One more floor,' Sack said puffing, his face flushed with perspiration.

Another zomb-proof door lay ahead. 'This is the penthouse, Johnny. This is where you're gonna die,' Griffin spat in my face.

The door swung back and revealed a huge apartment. The flick of a switch and spotlights illuminated everything. Unlike the rest of the building, this room appeared finished. Scenic artwork adorned the walls, and a set of sofas and chairs dominated the centre. One wall had a bar its entire length, with a neat row of optics lining the wall behind. The lounge area ran into an open plan kitchen, where expansive black granite worktops filled the space. No sign of the one person I wanted to see.

'You out did yourself,' I said to no one in particular.

'And you've ruined it,' Griffin shouted. 'My dream place now has a thousand dead people camping in the back garden.'

'I guess barbeques will be a bitch,' I said with a smile, making my head hurt worse.

'Yeah, laugh it up, Mr Policeman. Enjoy those last minutes on earth.'

'Where's Summer?'

'You are like a cracked record, Officer,' Jack said. 'I'll show you, shall I? Sack, bolt the door. I don't want any more visitors.'

The fat man obliged, and I was shoved towards the middle of three doors. Jack produced another key and my heart leapt a little. They were keeping something locked inside.

'Take a look for yourself,' Jack said and pushed me over the threshold. He flicked another light switch and I could see it was a bedroom. She was lying on her back and bound onto the bed. Summer wore nothing but torn underwear. Her mouth was gagged, just like the dead things in the barn. She thrashed at her binds as I rushed to help her. I looked down into face and wanted her to be alive. Her skin was milky-pale, but warm to the touch.

'You're alive,' I said.

'The things we did to her! All of us, Officer Johnny. Even Sack here had his fill, although he didn't last long,' Griffin told me.

Their guns were raised; they were expecting my reaction. One step forward and their fingers wrapped tight on the triggers. One half step closer and the windows exploded. A body tumbled in, then another in quick succession. The guns turned away from me. Wild, panicked shots filled the air.

I slammed the bedroom door closed on them and locked it. My hands worked on the ties and Summer was free. She pulled the gag away out of her mouth. 'Missed you,' she said.

'We need to run,' I pleaded, more shots ringing out. We went to the window and I pushed it up as far as it would go. The farmyard swarmed with the dead. The farmhouse to one side was over-run, body after body visible at every window.

I could now see how the dead had reached the penthouse window too. The vast numbers of dead surging against the rotten frame of the barn had caused it to sag and collapse against the new building. The fallen walls provided a way to climb up towards the lights and smells of the penthouse. There must have been thirty bodies on the wall, the living like a beacon to them.

'The roof is flat. We need to climb the gutters. Three feet and we're there,' I shouted back.

'Sounds the plan for me,' Summer answered me, pulling her clothes and shoes on.

'Are you okay? The things they said ...'

'Now is not the time, Johnny.'

I went first, grabbing at the plastic gutter and my shoes slipping for purchase. I reached wildly for grip, and felt myself begin to fall. Instinctively, I grabbed higher, feeling the muscles in my ribs begin to tear. Finally, I had the top ledge and for a second dangled by just one hand, before I managed to pull myself up. Lying exhausted on the flat bitumen roof, the stars winked down at me from the cloudless night sky.

'Summer,' I shouted down. 'It's not that bad!'

Reaching over for her, I braced myself the best I could. Fear was etched into her face as I pulled her towards me. To lose her now was no option at all. Kicking and scrambling, Summer joined me on the roof, our lips finding time to meet. 'I thought you were gone,' she said.

Looking around I wondered *where next?* More shots below followed by a shout. They knew we were out of the room.

'Block the roof access,' I shouted to Summer, and she put a spade handle through the hatch leading to the roof. 'It will slow them down at least.'

'We need another way down. Something they wouldn't expect,' I said.

'I know a way, although you won't like it,' she replied, taking me to the edge of the roof that faced the farmhouse. 'We run and jump the gap. Once we get onto that roof, I know there's a fire escape around the other side.'

'You know, long jump was my thing at school,' I said. The gap must have been ten metres, impossible on an even ground. We had height though, height to fall and make up the distance. 'I'll try first.'

'No, let's go together,' she said, as loud thumping came from the roof hatch. The wooden shaft began to splinter. A blast and there was a hole. 'Run!'

We held hands and sprinted. The air rushed past my face as we dropped. The impact on the other side was harsh, slates and guttering sheering off all around us. I felt Summer slipping towards the edge, and I grabbed out for her. Bob Sack was on the flat roof and shouting for his shotgun.

'We need to move. Now!' I shouted to Summer. A shot rang out and three slates to one side of us exploded into splinters and dust. Fragments raked the skin of my cheek. I put one hand on the chimney pot and we slid to the other side. The fire escape was filled with bodies, their hands already reaching for us. The garden below was near empty of dead. We had a chance.

'Fight or jump?' I called to Summer.

'Too far down,' she said and kicked out. The lead body fell back onto the step metal steps, taking two more like dominoes. 'Just keep kicking them.'

We did, and side by side, fought our way half way down, jumping the rest.

'Bravo,' Griffin said stepping out of the shadows. 'Aren't you two ready to join the fucking circus.'

We were on a raised piece of lawn, the scrubland behind us where Toby had been strung up and beaten. The bodies massed in the patio area below, straining to join us but balked by a simple metal gate.

'Stupid fucks, aren't they?' Griffin went on, and gestured for us to move. He marched us up the trail to Toby's tree, the darkness there almost liquid beneath the canopy of trees.

'No rope for hanging. More's the pity,' Griffin said. 'My old man would love this. But he's too busy dealing with the mess you made.'

He raised the shotgun. My hand reached out and found Summer's. A black figure walked slowly up behind Griffin. In one smooth movement, he wrapped arms around Griffin and sank his teeth into Griffin's neck. The shotgun barrel waved back and forth, discharging so close to us I felt the rush of pellets whizz by my face.

'Help me.'

We were running away. 'It was Bill, I'm sure it was Bill,' Summer shouted over. It was too dark to be sure. I tripped and fell every second stride as we went deeper into the woods.

'Which way?' I said. All around in the darkness I could hear stumbling, clumsy sounds. Bodies. Moving through the trees towards us. Finally, we had a path and ran faster. Around one corner an old woman lunged out, her cold hands touching mine. I pushed her away and we ran on. My heart jumped, the fear wanting to overwhelm me.

Breaking out of the woods, we made a clearing, and beyond there was the beach and incoming tide. It had been Lester's idea to attack the farm in the middle of the night. He had known when the tide would be high. I wished he was with us. The decline was steep, and we skidded and slid the last hundred feet down to the coastline. Pulling a metal lever on a steel gate, our feet finally crunched on the pebbles of the beach.

'We made it,' I said as we rounded the inlet to White Creek. Ahead was the yacht, sitting proud in the water, fifty feet off shore. 'My fault we didn't stash the canoe here too, there just wasn't the time. I guess we have ourselves a little swim.'

'Like I care about that. I love you, Johnny, don't ever forget that, okay?' Summer smiled.

We stripped some of our clothing off and held it above our heads. It was an ungainly swim, but at least it kept some things dry.

'Ow!' Summer said. 'Something touched me.'

'Swim faster, we're nearly there.'

Pulling out of the water was harder than I'd imagined. My limbs were tired and I felt like the water just wanted to suck us down. I found the handrail and then a step. Summer was behind me, her wet body pressing against mine. We flopped onto the deck like two freshly caught flounders.

'That was tougher than it looked,' I mouthed.

'I'll bring you some dry clothes from below,' Summer said.

I lay there staring up at the night sky again, comfortable and yet drowsy with fatigue. To just fall asleep would have been bliss. The tendrils of cloud passing over the half-moon were almost hypnotic. Five minutes passed.

'Summer, what are you doing?' I stood, feeling the boat shift in the water with my weight. 'We should cast off soon.'

Ducking my head I went below, my eyes taking time to adjust to the new darkness. 'Where are you Summer?' I felt my way towards the main bedroom. The door slid back, two people in the room.

'Nice of you to take the time to join us,' Jefferson's voice came out of the corner. He had a hunting knife to Summer's throat. 'One move, it's her, then you, okay?'

'What do you want?'

'I want to come with you, of course. The farm and the fence are gone. The village is finished. Summer tells me you want to go to that big oil rig out in the sea. It sounds like a damn good idea.'

'Put the knife down,' I said. 'We've all been through too much today already. You can come; it's no problem to us.'

'How do I know I can trust you?'

'I give you my word as a police officer. Just let Summer go.'

The knife went down and she rushed forward. I felt her muscles tremble. 'You are a bastard!' she spat back at Jefferson.

'I know,' he replied, the knife still pointing at us. "Just remember, I always have this.'

'We need to cast off, or we'll lose this tide,' I told him and turned us away. Back on deck, I pulled the drawstring on the outboard, and it started first time. Summer unhitched the buoy and we started to move away from the land. All three of us stood on the deck and watched the beach grow smaller. I counted five bodies on the shoreline, reaching out, watching us.

'Creepy bastards,' I muttered under my breath.

CHAPTER 33

Summer made an excuse, leaving Johnny and Jefferson on deck to unwrap the sails. She slipped into the cramped boat's toilet, her head woozy and faint. Part of her wanted to believe the feelings were only fatigue, that the trauma of the past few days had caught up with her, that all she needed was a little TLC and bed rest. The other part knew the truth.

Summer gazed at her petite hands, the nails she did her best to keep clipped and manicured. There was a palsy in them now, and the palms of her hands felt greasy. Her back felt hot and slippery with sweat, when there was no reason to be. Summer found the evidence at the bottom of her trouser leg, the tell-tale tear in material of her jeans. The material was tough, but had threaded and torn no more than a centimetre. She pulled the seam up and there it was, no more than a scratch, a break in her skin that meant only one thing. Thinking back she remembered the swim, how she had felt the nip on her leg. Now she knew, the tears filled up her eyes.

'What's wrong? What's wrong,' Johnny said to her as she went to him on deck. Her hands wrapped tight around him. She didn't want to speak. But time was short, and she knew she would say everything.

'I'm going to die, Johnny.'

'Don't be silly,' he said when she showed him. 'That's nothing, nothing at all.'

She watched his face, the beautiful face she had come to love. His look told her he knew, the hurt inside singing out through his eyes. He must feel the heat in her body, the furnace overload that came before the change. How many times had we all seen it happen, she wondered?

'We haven't got long now. Be careful not to kiss me.'

'I know.'

Summer felt herself guided back below, leaning more on him as her muscles did less. She caught an ugly look from Jefferson, the old man's spite and disgust. It tore her up to think Johnny would be left alone in the world with this man.

Laid down on the bed, she felt the quickening rise and fall of her breaths, her own body getting desperate for the oxygen to purge the sickness out.

'Do you think it will hurt?' she said.

'Should I help at the end?'

Summer didn't know how to answer. Her mind felt full of blank spots, a nothingness stealing her best memories. She wanted to drift away remembering all the good times they had together, but the sickness denied her even that. Instead, she satisfied herself with the touch of his hand, the smile on his face. How she wished there was more time to have. Perhaps in the next life?

'Come closer, you are too far away,' she said. 'You have to promise me.'

Johnny craned near, his ear almost touching her mouth. Her voice was getting faint as her throat died up. These would be her last words, she would make them count. When she had finished, Johnny stood back up and nodded. He had that serious look that sometimes made her laugh. She had always called it the 'two cogs at once' look to wind him up.

Johnny left the cabin door open and walked away. Summer heard voices, a discussion, a shout and a splash. Her eyes faded like a veil dropping down, her senses blinking out one by one. Would they come back later, she wondered?

A voice out in the dark, 'I love you.' Summer tried to smile one last time.

CHAPTER 34

The last of the boxes piled on the metal gangway around my feet, I sat and watched the yacht float from the docking area. It made a slow pirouette and then drifted towards the horizon. Summer's tomb would travel far away from here, to a better place, I decided. Tears dabbed on my sleeve, I began to carry the bags and boxes up the steel stairs to the next level.

I had been extremely lucky to moor the boat in the docking bay, and even with a gentle sea, the yacht had been badly dented and scraped against the giant pillars. No wonder they usually used helicopters to land on these mothers.

Looking high up the industrial tangle of girders and pipes, I could make out the red beacon that had captured Summer's and my imagination and had drawn us in. So many times we had sat on the beach and stared out to sea, thinking there could be a safer, better place for us. It was supposed to be me and Summer together. Life was so cruel.

Jefferson was gone. Summer had helped rid me of that man. She had given me the strength to toss him over the side, and watch him sink under a wave like the treacherous sack of shit he was. There would be no sleepless nights for him, I swore.

Breathing hard, I found myself on some kind of observation platform. Looking back, the mainland was nothing more than a hazy dream, an outline sketched by the faintest pencil. Jefferson's blade was in my hand now, my knuckles white as I turned the lever and pulled the door open. The air tasted stale and my empty stomach turned as another injection of adrenalin fizzed into my system. I was too tired for it to have a full effect, my legs like lead.

Pacing down the plastic laminate floor it was clear that this place was a maze, walkways and corridors spilling off in every direction. Turning down one I stopped, straining to hear movement, some other sign of life. It was clear there was still power in the building, the strip lights high on the walls glowing weakly. On a corner, I saw an arrow pointing to 'ENGINEERING', and followed. It crossed my mind I wouldn't be able to find my way back, but the urge to explore was too strong to resist. My grief for Summer numbed any fear I had.

'HELLO!' I found myself shouting randomly. No reply above the electrical hum in the walls.

At the double door to Engineering, I peered through wire mesh glass. Inside were a set of steep steps downwards, and the thumping drone of heavy machines. On the stairs, it was too noisy to think. I looked around myself constantly, waiting or perhaps even wanting to be attacked. Walking by the banks of machinery, I didn't know what a single one did. I guessed everything ran on automatic, like the windfarm.

The body flew at me from behind an oil tank. In a tattered blue boiler suit, he had been a big man with a beer belly. His big, grey hands grabbed me, slamming me backwards onto scalding metal pipes. My knees sank, equilibrium lost in my head, ears hearing only white noise. I was down, weakly pushing away this hellish man in front of me. The body's eyes were white and torn, two gaping holes in his face, the putrid smell I thought I'd left behind making me gag. The mouth was closing, this was my end I knew. Behind was a man in a suit, then nothing.

Drifting in space, I felt I was chasing faces. Spinning and tumbling high above the earth, I tried to catch them. My finger tips starting to catch fire, then my hands and my arms. The immense pain, then the face in the flames turned. It was my wife's face.

'I KNOW WHAT YOU DID.'

A booming voice sending me spinning and burning down to ground, my whole body a fireball, and the earth coming up and an end to it all.

'You were dreaming,' a woman said. 'A nightmare, I think.'

Blinking, my eyes started to focus. This was a medical room. I was lying on a gurney, shivering. There was an ache in my head, and in my arm too. I looked down and saw that I was attached to a drip.

'Where am I?'

'You're safe,' she said. I liked her smile. The woman was maybe forty years old, with short auburn hair. There were happy lines and creases around her eyes when she smiled. She wore round spectacles and a white lab coat.

'Lucky we got to you in time,' a second voice said, American sounding. I craned my neck towards the sound and made myself dizzy. In the corner of the room was a young man in a suit. Short, greased black hair; he looked strong and athletic. 'You're in our sickbay, my friend. I'm Trent and this is Alice.'

'Who the hell are you people?'

'Survivors, like yourself,' Trent answered. 'Lucky as hell to be here.'

'What about my things? I left them all out on the observation deck.'

'Don't worry, we found them while you were resting. We put them in your room for you,' Alice said, the smile again. 'Are you alone?'

'Yes,' feeling the bite of pain again.

'Tell us how you came to be here, friend,' Trent said. 'We're all ears.'

'Name's Johnny, a policeman from the mainland,' I said. I then proceeded to give them a potted history of what had happened, skipping Jefferson and one or two of the finer points. First impressions are everything, so they say.

'You and Summer were married?' Alice asked.

I looked down at the white patch of skin on my ring finger, the tell-tale sign of my past life and sins.

'Not to Summer. My wife was Kateyana; she left me before the outbreak.'

'Shit happens, man,' Trent said, squinting at me, studying.

'Sorry to come here uninvited. We never imagined there'd be other survivors. Not in a million years,' I said.

'Well, it's no problem; there are plenty of provisions. This place catered for a crew of a hundred when it was a fully operational rig. The best we have worked out is that most abandoned when the infection came, airlifted away back to the mainland. We fell lucky because the timing must have been at the start of one of their tours here. The larders are stocked full of food, enough for the three of us for a very long time. The downside you experienced yourself. Below decks, in the engineering levels and venting shafts, there's still plenty of those monsters left,' Alice explained.

'Cunning fucks too. Awkward to flush out in all those levels down there. We do our best. Lucky for you we followed you, or that fat fuck would have dined out on you all day.'

'So how did you two end up here yourselves?' I asked. There was something in Alice's eyes, uncertainty I thought. It itched at me.

'We were just tourists on our holidays, caught a boat at just the right time. It must be crazy on the mainland right now,' Trent said, quick to butt in.

I held his stare. 'It has its moments.'

'You should rest,' Alice said. 'I'll bring you some food later.'

'Okay.'

They seemed glad to leave the room.

CHAPTER 35

There was a sound, a low hiss of water jetting out of a tap, then a splash of something in water. Steam flowed out beneath my bathroom door, not a little but a whole sauna room full. I tried to swipe the white smoke away from my face, feeling the sweat prickle beneath my clothing as I walked inside. My fingers touched the cold porcelain of a white sink, and drew a mark across the steamed up mirror above.

Another splash. Turning, the steam billowed up around me and I opened my eyes wide to see. There was a bath in the centre of the room, four feet in the shape of lion's paws. It looked like a museum relic, huge and smooth around the rims. My wife Kateyana was in the bath, and she was smiling at me.

'It's been a long time since we've seen each other,' the English rough around her musky Scandinavian accent. The long black hair looked heavy and soaked. She was close enough for me to see the three grouped moles on her shoulder. The mole field I had once said. Her ribs looked too prominent, and her bust barely more than a young boy's. How she had loved to starve herself. But there was beauty too. I had forgotten that, and the reminder stung.

'It been a long time, John,' Kateyana said. 'Too many adventures, too many distractions. I'm back now.'

'But you left.'

'Is that what you like to tell yourself, John?' And she sank down below the rich foam bubbles in the water. She disappeared.

I plunged my hands down into the depths. The bath was bigger than before, a vast pool, spreading around me. I found her, pulled her to the surface, blinded by the soap and the bubbles.

She made me scream.

'Do you not love me anymore?' Kateyana said, her skin the colour of rancid meat, maggots living in her skin. A smile split her cheeks, jawbone and gristle.

I woke in the dark. My body hot, headache in my temples.

'I would have woken you up earlier, but you looked so peaceful. We all get nightmares sometimes here. All perfectly natural. Now come, you must be starving,' Alice said, looking down on me.

My arm throbbed when she removed the cannula and drip. She led me by the hand to the canteen. I felt in a daze.

What did you dream about?'

'I don't remember,' I lied.

'This is our little store cupboard,' Alice said.

She was joking. The food storage area stretched thirty feet at least. Metal framed shelves lined the centre and both walls, and they were stacked high with all manner of tins, packets and boxes, every one of them non-perishable items. We had an Aladdin's cave and I wished Summer could have seen it. I picked up one tub that read POWDERED EGGS. 'Any good?'

'Better than you'd think. Do you want a fry up? There's some irradiated sausages around here somewhere I think,' she laughed.

'I'll settle for a little cereal, thanks.'

Trent joined us in the canteen area. There must have been enough seating for a hundred people. The three of us sat on one table, just a couple of strip lights lit, the rest of the tables in shadow. It was quiet, with nothing but the dull clank of cutlery on our plate, and our intermittent, clipped conversation.

'So you're real police are you Johnny?' Trent said. He'd changed into combat pants, boots and was wearing a light-weight black stab vest. 'Hope you can handle a firearm. I know you guys like to wing and a prayer it when it comes to bad guys. In the NYPD, they shoot you for jay walking.'

'Not an offence around here, Trent,' I said.

'No offences a man can't get away with these days. Isn't that right, Alice?' he nudged. 'Anyway, I've got a present for you. I think you'll like.'

Trent pushed a new looking Glock across the table towards me. Picking it up it felt very light and plastic. I dropped the magazine and saw it was fully loaded.

'Nice weapon; where did you find it?'

'So many questions, Johnny. You know there's no police anymore, don't you? I took it off a dead guy on the mainland,' Trent said.

'You seem awfully well equipped, Trent, for a tourist,' I said. Alice looked sheepish again; a poor poker player.

'What can I say, Johnny, I was an eagle scout when I was a kid,' Trent said, and changed the subject. 'Anyway, business of the morning. Now you are rested you should know that everything that glitters isn't necessarily gold. We got us a few issues here on the rig, well one main issue actually. Dead people keep turning up like bad pennies from down below. It seems we aren't half as unpopulated as first we thought. Fucking sucks, but the order of the day is to get those bodies before they come up here spoiling our little party. I for one am sick of sleeping with one eye open, if you know what I mean. And now we got ourselves some real, honest-to-goodness law enforcement, I want us all to sort this problem once and for all.'

'What Trent means in his longwinded, charmless way is we'd be really grateful if you could help us kill a few more of those dead things,' Alice said.

'Fine by me,' I said.

Later, I found myself on the metal stairs in Engineering, the Glock in my hand. Trent was on point with a pump action shotgun, vague again when talking about its source. Alice followed behind with a steel pipe, eyes hard. We walked down a level, unable to hear each other from the noise of machinery. I spotted the area where I had been attacked. There was nothing there now other than a black smear of blood on the laminate. Alice mimed throwing something overboard, and I figured they must have disposed of the body whilst I was asleep.

We went past the stain and found another set of metal stairs. Looking down, all I could see was level upon level of machinery. The heat coming up was oppressive. I remembered my old sergeant, Dolan, talking about this place. He had called it a super-rig, a new design. At first hand, the scale was terrifyingly immense.

Trent indicated to me to keep my eyes open and we went down. Sweat ran into my eyes, and I wiped it away on my sleeve. There seemed more pipes than machines, the further we went. Five levels down Trent spread his arms. I took it to mean they hadn't checked this far before. Steam hissed and half the lights seemed to have a flicker about them, as if they were going to die any second. Looking around, I didn't see any movement.

Following Trent onto the walkway, I saw the first body. It was crawling out from a data bank machine, a thin man with thinning hair in another grey overall. Must have been Maintenance or Engineering in life I guessed. One side of his face had the constitution of burnt hamburger, as if he'd pressed it against one of the scalding pipes and not even noticed his face frying off. The man crawled because one leg was missing from below the left knee, chewed or torn away.

The body started grasping its way towards us. Trent had some sort of combat knife in his hand. He neatly

210

stepped over the man's hands and thrust it down through the back of his head. The *grunching* sound was just audible over the din in the pipes, and then Trent was away. Part of me wondered just who I was dealing with here, either a martial arts nut or some kind of ex-military. Stepping over the corpse, I saw the semi-severed head's eyes still following me. God, I hated it when that happened!

The walkway led us around the corner. Over the side of the railing, I could see the twelve levels below. Flashes of movement in the shadows, more dead personnel than I could count.

We dropped another level, and my spine tingled. Trent seemed to be rushing, and I wondered what we had left above us. The thought crossed my mind that we could be surrounded, that we could easily all die in the bowels of this oilrig. Looking back at Alice I caught the look of anxiety on her face, before her face creased back into a broad smile. She could fake those smiles well, I thought, even the lines around her eyes appeared genuine. Trent made a pushing sound with his hands and we were ducking into a low ceiling tunnel lined with thin pipes. The back of my hand accidently brushed over one. I jerked it away expecting it to be burnt, instead the pipe was stone cold.

Trent was far ahead and, distracted, I didn't see the hand until it was too late. Dirty fingers grabbed me by the hair. Small boned hands. The child was lying on the pipes above me, then rolled off and knocked me off my feet. Trying to push her off, I was trapped by the confined space of the walkway tunnel. The girl was maybe ten years old, her face bloated and puffed with decay. I saw her needle teeth darting at my face. I shoved at her, the Glock lost. The demon had my hair. Lunging, I saw Alice strike her once in the back of the head with the pipe. I slid free, the girl limp and still.

Stumbling back I found myself standing back on the walkway, the noise of machinery drowning my senses. Alice and Trent came out of the darkness of the tunnel together. I spread my hands at Trent, a violent gesture. He shrugged his shoulders, bemusement on his face. His time would come, I thought, and walked away. My breaths were tight gulps as I made my way back up the metal staircase.

CHAPTER 36

'And that's Rummy,' Alice said.

Taking another slug of the dirty rum, I stared at my cards. A jumble of suits, well beaten. 'Another one?'

'Okay, but we can change games if you've had enough. I play a mean Texas Hold 'em as well,' she said.

'Poker better with more people, isn't it? Where has Trent disappeared to now?' I said, looking around the lounge room we'd settled into.

'Trent's a bit like a ghost. Always heading off to haunt someplace or other, jangling his chains.'

'So what is the connection with you two? How did you end up with that guy?'

'Long story,' she said looking away.

'I thought he said you were tourists, on your holidays when the outbreak came? Trent did well to find himself so much hardware, and then get you both all the way over to this rig. Impressive!'

'You can tell you were a cop in a past life. You want to know my life story and we only just met. What if we were to turn the tables? I heard you calling out a name last night. Kateyana? Who was this person? It was Summer on the boat, no?' The smile again.

It was my turn to shift awkwardly in my seat. She was right, I didn't like it one bit. 'Kateyana was my wife.'

'Ah, you said you didn't remember what you dreamed about. I guess we all like little secrets, Johnny,' Alice said, dealing out the cards onto the table.

'My wife left me. She moved away to London with a younger man. She hated the country, she hated me too.'

'Don't look so serious, I was only teasing. Nobody is free of these dreams I think,' her eyes sparkling beneath the lenses of her glasses.

I raked more pound coins towards my pile. Money, good for nothing but counters. 'Better at poker,' I said, as I hit my second flush. 'So have you only been with Trent since the outbreak? Knight in shining armour and all that.'

'Longer,' she said. 'We met at a demonstration years ago. G8 Summit in Glasgow 2005. Riot cop had barged me into a lamppost with his shield. Blood all down my face, I didn't know what the hell was going on. And there he was to save me.'

'G8 was all about climate change, wasn't it?' I said, but Trent entered the room and distracted us.

'Zombie nearly got up to our level. Got to watch those fucks all the time,' he said, making a big show of cleaning off his big knife. 'Beginning to think your idea is better. Build ourselves a fence or a barrier to stop them getting up the walkways. Rot the fuckers out.'

So that's what we did. Not a tidy, high tensile fence like Jack's, but an untidy heap of filing cabinets and other assorted office furniture launched to the bottom of the tunnel level. It was hard work, but by the end of the day, we had all four main staircases blocked. If any bodies still lurked higher up, at least they would be slim in number and more easily dealt with.

'How is this place still running?' I asked Trent, as we left Engineering.

'Beats me,' he said. 'Runs on automatic, who are we too argue with that. My dear old Ma once said, if it ain't broke, don't fix it. The rule is, don't go pressing buttons.'

'So are you army or something, back in the States?'

'What makes you say that?'

'The guns, the knives. A guy's got to wonder how a tourist got so well armed.'

'I was never in the army, Johnny. Don't believe in those big institutions. When I was young, I just watched a lot of Arnie and Sly doing their thing, know what I mean?'

'If you say so, Trent.'

Looking at his bulk walk away, I didn't know what to think. He was hard to know, harder to trust. And what of Alice, and her fake smiles?

Time went on, days blended into weeks. Alice and I worked our way through every board game we could lay our hands on, marking time. Trent continued to drift in and out, spending time alone beyond the barriers we made. Sometimes we'd hear a gun shot echo up through the superstructure, another body at the end of a bullet. At night the dreams came on fast, turning my single bed into a pool of sweat. Often I'd wake and see Alice standing in the doorway, watching. Other nights my mind would play cruel tricks. It would be Kateyana in the doorway, edging closer, her arms outstretched and reaching for me.

Stepping up to the mirror, I used the electric shaver recklessly, leaving tufts of bristle behind. My bloodshot eyes told a story of sleepless nights. Guilt leaving lines in my skin, making me appear older. No youth left to savour.

Leaving my shoes off, I walked towards the canteen until I heard their voices. Back the way I had come, Trent and Alice's room was a level above. The door was closed and I tried the handle. Looking back along the long corridor, I felt I was being watched, that at any second they were going to be running for me, shouting my name. The handle gave and I went inside. The bedroom was bright with sunlight, air fresh from the open window. Outside the waves whipped up white tips.

I started to open drawers. Socks, lots of socks! Three drawers, and nothing to show. I went elsewhere. In the corner of the room was a metal locker. The padlock was a problem. I went to the bedside cabinet. Condoms, pens and chewing gum, I felt like some kind of pervert for even looking. I paused a moment, worried I might be hearing footsteps. In the old days I'd need a warrant to even thinking of doing a search like this. And what was I looking for? I didn't even know. No magistrate would have given me the time of day.

I pulled out assorted magazines and books, a thin film of dust on top of them. Sifting through the pile, long dead celebrity faces stared up at me. I wondered if out on the streets of London was a zombie version of Jordan, flaunting her giant, rotten chest and devouring any man she came across. Could you even tell the difference?

Throwing back the bed sheets there was nothing to see. Sighing, I knew I was out of time. There was a jacket on the floor, one of Trent's combat style affairs. Going through the pockets my fingers felt a plastic bag. Bringing it into the light I saw a name, YALE. At the bottom, like a little silver tadpole, was a spare key. I dropped the padlock to the floor and yanked the cabinet door. It was empty.

Trent must keep his weapons locked in here, I thought. Safe habits, or perhaps just keeping them out of my hands. I'd never got the Glock back after I dropped it in the tunnel. I was about to close the cabinet door and swept my hand over the top shelf, not expecting to find anything. But there was something. I slipped it off the shelf; a photograph, a group of military types standing and kneeling to fit in the frame. Nearly everyone held a gun in their hands and wore a mishmash of clothes. No one person in the same uniform. Alice and Trent were standing together on the second row. Their faces were blank, staring into the distance. Written on the bottom of the photograph was one word in red, *Ragnorak*. I knew what I had to do now.

CHAPTER 37

It was sunny outside. The sausages sizzled on the disposable barbeque Alice had found. I turned them, making room for my burger. The two of us sat on a platform high on the rig, barren paint-chipped metal surrounding us as if we were in the palm of some giant colossus. A huge cylinder behind acted as a break from the insistent north-westerly winds. My eyes relaxed looking out over the rolling sea.

'Will Trent be joining us?' I asked.

'He's busy at the moment I think, doing his thing down below. Told me he was making real progress with the bodies, that he's close to clearing the last clusters,' her hand playing with her hair, a new nervous tick.

'That's nice,' I answered. 'So what did you two do again after university?'

'Oh I don't know, travelled a lot. Took our share of shitty jobs. You know the usual Johnny. Why are you digging again?'

'Just passing the time,' I said.

Nothing was going to be achieved with simple conversation, I knew that. Looking at Alice I didn't see laughter lines or a kindly manner anymore; there was something beneath that. It was her hands that gave her away. Hard calluses and dry skin. I felt them when she held my hand. There was a fighter hidden behind her sweet face, a whole life beyond idle chat around a smoking barbeque.

'I forgot something,' I lied. 'I'll be back in a minute.'

Closing the watertight door behind me, I ran, falling round corners and bouncing off walls all the way to Engineering. Trent's kit bag lay next to the door. He used it to carry his precious guns here before each trip down. I rooted through the zip pockets, and found what I wanted.

The spare Glock had a full magazine, I pressed off the safety catch and started through the din of the engine rooms. Ungainly, I climbed over the barrier of furniture, nearly losing the gun when the filing cabinet tipped and crashed over. *So much for the surprise.*

Passing through the tunnel, I eyed the body of the girl carefully, congealed blood around her crumpled form sticky under the soles of my boots. On the other side I looked out across an unfamiliar network of walkways and stairs. Trent was here somewhere. I wondered if he was watching me now. Taking the first steps down, I came to a smaller, rusted walkway, the heat and the noise intensifying as if we were inside of one giant engine. There was a circular hole, a metal ladder going twenty feet down. The lights were flickering and dim. I thought it was empty, but I wasn't sure.

By halfway down, I knew I was an idiot, even before the hand grabbed my ankle and sent me flat onto my back. Dazed and winded, I stared into an angry face, spittle caught and hanging on the edge of his lips.

'What the fuck were you thinking?' Trent said. 'Where the hell is Alice?'

'I'm ...' I managed, before he dragged me to my feet and pulled me into a side room. I'd lost the gun.

'It's not safe out there, you shouldn't have come.'

I looked around and found my feet again. There was a bank of dead computers all along one side of the room. Another larger table at the far end sat next to a swivel leather chair. On the table was a laptop and a cable leading off, connecting to the mains. Trent's water canteen and favourite brand of nuts were on the table too. This was his workstation. I walked towards it, and felt Trent's hand grab my sleeve.

'What's with the laptop, Trent? I thought all the communications were dead?'

'Just games. I come down here for some peace and quiet.'

In the window behind Trent, I saw a body shuffling closer. A woman in life, perhaps a cleaner or cook for the rig, who knew? Torn and rotten, she hadn't noticed us yet.

Pulling away from Trent, I marched up to the laptop. Pressing a key, it asked for a password. Above it in red letters read *Ragnorak*. 'What does this all mean Trent?'

'It means you shouldn't poke your nose where it doesn't belong,' he answered, the Glock now pointing at my head.

'I know it translates as apocalypse, Trent, I just don't know why you and Alice need a code word. I saw the picture as well; I know you're not tourists. So that begs the question … who the hell are you really Trent?'

'You're a long way from your jurisdiction, Johnny. I don't have to answer your prissy questions,' Trent said, gun hand tense.

'I don't think you come down here to play games, Trent. I don't see you as a game player at all. No, you're using this to talk to somebody. Do you know something about how this happened?' I said, a half-step closer.

'Going to your grave not knowing, I wonder if in the afterlife you'll sit there frustrated?'

The gun twitched, sweat beaded on Trent's top lip. I braced myself, my muscles tensed. The window exploded behind and the shot went wide. The woman sent Trent spinning off balance. Heavy set, she had him pinned to the ground. I kicked his gun hand and evened the fight. The Glock spun into space, fingers broken. Trent tried to wrestle her head away, but she was good. She'd done this before. 'Help me!'

Looking down, I shouted at him, 'What did you do?' But too late, his neck was open. Trent's blood was a fountain to the ceiling. I reached for a weapon, blood slippery underfoot. The woman turned to me, preferring the living to the dead. At point blank range, I decorated the blood-red walls with her brains. Bagging Trent's other weapons and his laptop, I was out before any more bodies traced the sounds. There was one person left who would answer my questions.

CHAPTER 38

'Where did you get to?' she said. 'Thought I'd have to send out a search party.'

I stood in front of Alice, the gun bag stashed away. Part of me wondered what I must look like. Could I simply smile and hide everything that had just happened? The blood washed out, but I felt death had soaked into me. I watched the rich laughter lines spread across her face. I tried to mirror her.

'Making tea. You thirsty, Johnny?'

'Sure,' I said. 'Gasping.'

She arranged three mugs on the counter. Tea for Alice and me, the coffee for Trent. It was a waste.

'I thought we could defrost the gammon from the freezer. It will help us use up the pineapple can you opened.'

'Sure, why not,' I answered. 'Where has Trent got too?'

'He promised he would be back by three. Must have found something that needs his special attention.'

'Quite the hunk your man, isn't he?'

'He can scrub up. Shame I don't have a sister to introduce you to. Do you get a bit lonely, Johnny? The oil rig gooseberry?'

'Alice, I need to ask you a few things.'

'Trent will be here soon, he's better with the question stuff,' she answered.

'Alice,' I said, snapping her attention back. 'I need to know how you really ended up here.'

'I told you already, we were tourists. We found a boat, we were lucky to get away,' she answered, a nervous look at the door.

'He's not coming Alice, so please stay focused. Time for the truth.'

'I don't know what's got into you today. What do you mean about Trent?' She started to walk for the door.

'Alice, this isn't a game. I want the truth,' I repeated, grabbing the crook of her elbow and turning her.

'What the hell ... I am going to find Trent. You can't stop me.'

'I saw the picture, Alice. You're not a tourist. Start from the beginning.'

'You ever play paintball, Johnny?'

A pause and then she dashed for the door. I dived and made an awkward tackle. We both sprawled to the floor, my shoulder slamming into the door frame. Blinding pain.

'Proud of yourself Johnny?' I heard her say. 'Hitting girls.'

'Get up and go and sit down,' I said, straightening up. I saw the screwdriver before I felt the pain, a two inch point in her hand. She made two puncture wounds before I even got chance to react. 'Bitch!'

A knuckle popped as I drove it into her nose. It flattened to one side, an ugly squash. Alice's eyes rolled back, and she fell in a heap. My hand went instinctively to my side, hot, red blood flowing out. I grabbed an old towel off the canteen worktop and pressed it hard into the wound. The rag was instantly crimson.

Alice began to stir on the canteen floor, moaning and gurgling with the blood in her throat. Taking her hair, I dragged Alice back to her chair. My blood pooled at my feet as I took the cord strips out of my pocket and tied her down. I'd known from leaving Trent this would be my only way to get the truth. Never expected to get stabbed though.

'Wake the fuck up,' I shouted, slapping her cheek.

'What the fuck did you do, Johnny?' Her voice was distorted by a nasal slur.

'I'm asking the questions. The group in the picture, who are you?'

'I wanna speak to a lawyer,' she said with a defiant smile. The lines working, despite the damage. 'The wounds will kill you, Johnny. You should let me take a look.'

'Who are you?'

'You should work more on that interrogation technique, Officer Silverman.'

The next slap broke the skin on the corner of her mouth. 'You need to start giving me something.' The effort made me dizzy.

'Trent will be here soon,' she answered. 'You better be ready to run.'

'Trent is ... somewhere safe. But, I can assure you that he won't be making your three o'clock appointment. However, if you give me something then I might consider feeding him later. Ragnorak? Let's start with that.'

Her eyes narrowed, she stared me out, a different person. 'Ragnorak was a code name for the end. Stupid name if you ask me.'

'So the government knew about this disease before it happened? Are they all in bunkers?'

'You really don't get it do you, Johnny? We're not the government, Johnny. They were caught with their pants down same as everyone else. We are independent of anybody's rule. We did this for our planet, Johnny.'

'What the hell are you talking about? No one could make the whole world turn upside down. You want me to believe you and those people in the picture did all this?'

'Tip of the iceberg,' Alice said, a blood bubble coming out the side of her broken nose. 'Ragnorak was the name for a collective of people who believed in global warming. Global groups with similar concerns talking

223

through internet forums, nothing wrong with that. But, out of that came the militant side, the ones that never believed the governments would ever give more than lip service to the boiling of our world, Johnny. We thought there would never be change until it was far too late. That the people of this earth would continue to belch out carbon dioxide like it was going out of fashion. I've never been what you would call a people person, deep down, Johnny.' She laughed and grimaced.

'How the hell can a bunch of environmentalist freaks cause the nightmare I've been living for the last six months?'

'We had a scientist; his name was Hilton. He made something that we could put in the water. I don't know how but it worked on the neuro-system. It shut down organs, ruined people's brains. We were told it would kill people who drank it, end them cleanly, with no pain. It was designed to be invisible, to pass through water treatment works into people's taps undetected. Somewhere along the line, it must have mutated, or maybe someone wanted this to happen all along. There were thousands of activist cells all over the world, people who really care about the world. Trent and I were part of a team of four who attacked a water works on a coast. Unfortunately, by morning we were fighting zombies to survive, the other two in the group turned into those things. We were given injections; promised we would be immune. Placebos, I guess. Trent found the rig for us to wait it out, ready to start the world again. We did it to save the future, Johnny.'

'You killed everyone I loved, Alice. How are you going to make that right again?'

'There can't be any going back, Johnny. There will be enough people left to start again, but global warming will end. The planet will be safe for the future. No more selfish destruction.'

'You've killed billions of people, Alice,' I said, woozy now. 'There's nobody left to thank you.'

'When I die, my conscience will be clean. How is your conscience, Johnny? I've heard you talk about your wife in your sleep. Kateyana was it ... what happened to her?'

'She died, like nearly everyone else.' It was a brush off. In my mind, I could see the bath.

'I told you everything, Johnny. Get Trent here from wherever you're holding him. Show me that he is safe,' she said, in tears now.

'One more thing first,' I said, putting Trent's laptop on the table. 'Is this how your cells communicate?'

I jogged down the corridor, a blood-sodden bandage wrapped tight around my middle. Trying to focus, I stopped to look at a wall map, finding where I was in the maze of levels and walkways. My bloodied fingers traced a path to the room I wanted. The Emergency Room, an apt description I thought. Jogging on I hoped to find a life raft, someway to return to the mainland. I couldn't live with a woman who would undoubtedly kill me, or alone where madness would creep up and have me whole. Better to go back, feel the earth under my feet again. The rig was a mirage, a stilted nightmare. I wanted no part of it anymore.

The door opened, and I fumbled for the light switch. The sidelights came on casting out red gloom. Main lights seemed inoperable. I moved past the hanging all-weather rubber suits, baggy wet suits for the workers who had to work outside in the lashing North Sea weather. Next to one of the lockers I found one of the things I'd come for, a packaged inflatable life raft. I tried it for weight, heavy but moveable. On the packaging, it warned it would explosively inflate. I dragged it out to the centre of the room, and started to pile in the things I would need.

225

The door into the room slammed open making me jump. A body crashed in, more running than walking. It was moving faster than any zombie I'd seen before. I hurled a metal locker over and ran around the corner of the room. There was no way through, a painted breezeblock wall and no door. In my confusion, I couldn't even remember where I'd left the Glock. The body snarled its way nearer, I recognised it now in the harsh light. The wound in Trent's neck was still raw and fresh, the black eyes and dead skin showed life's spark had snuffed out. He bared his teeth and sprang for me.

No time to react, he barrelled into me. Trent bounced me off the wall and drove me painfully off my feet. Strong in death, as he had been in life, Trent over-powered my arms and looked to sink his teeth in. I brought my knee up full force and caught his head with a glancing blow. I staggered up as Trent recouped and came again. Kicking out, I missed, then blindly ran up one side of the room. Trent was so fast, he was already ahead, blocking the exit. He lunged in again, teeth snapping next to my face, breath rank. My fist found his face, my knuckles screaming with pain. I might as well have been hitting a shop mannequin for all the effect it had.

My breaths were getting shorter, insides not right, punctured and broken. I faced him again, my hands pushing his mouth up from under his chin, trying to keep his mouth closed. We rotated in the centre of the room, our dance of death. My strength was fading, time for me to give up. Would we stumble back to where Alice sat tied up, each taking turns to pick her bones clean?

My vision was in and out, the light more black than red. Buckling, I fell back with Trent on top of me. The objects felt familiar, my hand reaching out and grasping a plastic cylinder. My other hand was slipping from his jaw. Trent forced his mouth down towards me, an open chasm trying to swallow me whole. I forced the cylinder upwards into his mouth. Pulling the toggle, Trent's mouth erupted into a volcanic show, a supernova of burning light. The fire from the flare took his head, and I crawled away.

The flailing creature that was Trent flung itself around the room, clothing alight. I ran back out into the corridor, hit a fire alarm for sprinklers, but no water came. Fire quickly spread to the ceiling. I ran down the corridor, licking flames following. Around a corner, three dead bodies. They found a purpose and moved towards me. Trent must have dislodged the barriers.

Changing direction, I ran for an external door. Cold air hit my face, as behind me I heard the shatter of glass, yellow flames spreading over the super-structure. Another explosion, close enough that I felt the metal walkway under my feet move and start to give way. At the edge, I found the steps down. There was no time left.

Trying to climb down the ladder the dizziness gripped, and then I was falling. The shock of the water woke me, and I flailed to resurface in the freezing sea, drawing breath as the rig burned above like a Roman candle. Somewhere inside the fire Alice was burning too, for her sins and what she did to us all. I paddled slow backstrokes away towards the night horizon. Directionless, I had no idea where the land lay. Too far anyway. I knew these would be my last hours.

CHAPTER 39

I saw her face, clear as if she was in front of me. There was Kateyana's harsh Scandinavian beauty undressing before me, steam rising from the boiling bath water. She had always liked it that way, hotter than hell. I used to say it was because she had ice in her veins, that she needed to thaw them out. Once upon a time, she had liked that.

Her mouth was moving, but no sound was there. It was if I had to tune in somehow, to hear her words clearly.

'I don't think I can stay like this any longer. Once upon a time, I thought we were so alike. Now I know, Johnny, you just don't believe in anything. Not a single thing.'

'I believe in you.'

'I don't mean the simple things, Johnny. Where's your passion for anything? Art or music, all the important things I love?'

'What's going to happen to us?'

'I am going to move out, Johnny, move away from this nasty village. I'm drowning in it. I hate it.'

'Let me come with you.'

'No, you stay here and rot Johnny.'

Looking down on her, I wondered if this would be the last time I'd ever see her lily white body, the firm but soft contours I would caress for hours. 'I have to come with you.'

'I haven't said all yet ... I don't know how. There's somebody else, Johnny. It hurts so much to tell you these things. I wish it wasn't like this.'

'Why can't you stop then?' I said reaching down, just to touch her.

'Don't,' she said, brushing my hand off. 'It doesn't feel right anymore. Can you leave my bathroom? I want my old life back.'

'But I love you,' I said, lost in tears now.

'You know things haven't been right, I don't know if they ever were Johnny. We were young ...'

'Who is this man, Kateyana? Do I know him?'

'Why do you assume? Why does it have to be a man? Perhaps I want a woman who actually has emotions, that doesn't just pretend all the time. When do you ever see my friends? You just want to stay in this awful little job, your dead end existence.'

'I'm a policeman, Kateyana; I help people.' My hands above her soft shoulders. They pushed down, life in them of their own. Her face went under the water, oddly easy. I ignored the kicking feet, the hot splash of the water, all the time watching her face. Sinking down, I sat against the bath and wondered what I had done. There would be a trial; I would live a life in shame. There would be beating when other inmates found out who I was, and what I had done. There was no part of me that could live with that.

My knowledge had saved me in the short term. I took her remains and burned them in an old clay kiln that I knew of, hidden in the woods near Haven. Scraping out the brittle bones a day later, I smashed them to dust with a hammer. The residue was given to the sea; there was nothing left of Kateyana. I took her things out of my house and burnt those too. I told everyone she had left. Eventually friends and family would ask questions. Eventually I would be doomed, I knew that. I waited for the other shoe to drop, but instead the world ended around me, just another murderer in the new barbarous world.

My eyes opened and I was floating. My limbs numb from the cold water, the rising sun on the horizon. The rig was a burnt cinder, the structure sagging down on its supports back into the sea. Small fires still raged, melting metal like butter. There would be no going back.

I saw a body in the water fifty feet away, bobbing and twitching. It was undead, and I swam lashing strokes away from it. Part of me wondered why I hadn't died already, the cold had numbed my limbs so much that I wasn't even sure where the stab wounds were anymore. Closing my eyes, I stopped paddling, letting the roll of the waves carry me. I wanted to dream again, to be carried away again. A noise kept interrupting my thoughts, like a buzz of a wasp. My eyes wouldn't focus. There was something in the water above me, then a voice.

'Did they not teach you to wear a life jacket at police school?'

Lester.

He pulled me aboard and I lay immobile in the dinghy, like a freshly caught flounder gasping for air.

'How did you …' I managed before exhaustion took hold.

The sea spray roused me, already the sun had climbed high into the sky. Sitting up, my head swum and the small fishing boat rocked.

'Easy, Johnny,' Lester said, his hands wrapped round the outboard throttle.

Blinking, I looked away, sighting the land maybe a mile and a half ahead. I recognised the distinctive shape of coves and inlets. We had a course dead set for Haven.

'I thought you were dead, Lester.'

'Perhaps I am just a figment of your dying imagination, or a sea demon taking you away for a lifetime of torment,' Lester said. 'No, that gunshot didn't kill me. Just a flesh wound then a lot of pain tweezing all that buckshot out. It turned out those farmers made their own DIY shotgun shells. I got a bit lucky and got the fine stuff shot into me. It did manage to knock me out for a while though. Some nice scars.' He showed me the dimple marks below his ribs.

'Chicks will dig those,' I said.

'That Alison, Jack's little lady, helped me with it. She's a kind woman.'

The full horror of what Summer and I had run away from came back to me, the dead overrunning everything.

'What the hell happened after we left, Lester?'

'I won't butter it up for you Johnny. When I came to, I woke in the dark. Thank God, it wasn't the barn. That rotten lump of wood collapsed against the new building and climbed up like ants, didn't they? No, I woke up in the generator room. And I hadn't got there by magic either. That angel, Alison had seen everything and dragged me out of harm's way. Some kind of miracle it was! She saw the mess my stomach was, and got me on my feet again. By dawn we even dared look outside; world flipped upside down.'

'There must have been hundreds, maybe a thousand zombies, Lester. Why the hell are you steering us back there?' I shouted over to him, trying to make details on the distant shore. It was too far to see clearly.

'Well here's the rub of it, Johnny, there wasn't half as many of those dead, walking types as you would have expected. Turns out after Griffin was killed, Jack took it badly. The man fought through the masses and mounted a tractor. He started bellowing, flashing every light and headlight he had on that thing and led 'em out of that gap in the fence again like he was some kind of damn pied piper! Man went and martyred himself. The men blocked up the hole we blew in the fence and started about culling the dead folk we still had left inside the village perimeter. There were still a lot of casualties; I said I wouldn't butter it up none, but in the end we got 'em all. We had our peace again.'

'So what about the farmers, Lester?'

'They're done; dead, every last one of them. We actually found the dead version of Griffin sat with his brother Dexter in the ruins of the barn. They looked kind of happy together in a sick kind of way, brotherly love and all that. We shot them in the head without a second thought. Nobody left in the village now 'cept the good folk. That's why you can go back, start again. There must be about sixty people left, hanging on just fine. Sorry Summer's not here, liked her a lot.'

'How did you find me, Lester? I was as good as dead out here.'

'I'd watched the rig from the beach for weeks, that distant flashing red light. Kind of liked the fact you had made it. Figured you may come back one day if the food ran out. I kept the fact of your whereabouts to myself, a man needs a few secrets. I considered joining you, but old Lester likes the earth under his feet best. Then last night I saw the flames, knew there must have been trouble. Took the boat at dawn to see what could be done. Lucky I did ...'

The beach was close; I remembered it from the dead seal so long ago. It felt like years, but I knew it was only six or seven months. On the outside, I'd had a life and a job, everything was superficially right to the observer. But I remembered how I had really felt, the shadow of the murder hanging over me, colouring everything with darkness. Now the world would never ask the right questions. I would never be tried and there would be no justice for Kateyana. It had cost the whole world to make me a free man. Looking at the empty beach, I felt a wave of warmth on my skin.

'Peaceful, ain't it?' Lester said.

A flicker of movement caught my eye as I waded to shore. Looking over, I saw something run out onto the rocky beach then dart back into the small caves in the small cliff face. Just a rabbit.

'So where have you been living ...' I began to say, but something in Lester's face stopped me dead. There was a tension, something was wrong. Then I saw them creeping along the beach, hunched down, villagers with guns. A group of ten or more was coming one way down the beach, I looked the other way and there was at least as many again. More started to come out of the woods above the cliff path, and behind I heard the hum from more than one outboard motor. Completely surrounded; we had no choice but to stand and wait.

Leading the group from one side of the beach was Jack Nation. 'What have you done to me, Lester? You said he was dead.'

'Officer Silverman, so good of you to join us again. We really had no idea you were sunning yourself out on that oilrig until Lester let it slip last night. If I'd known, we would have visited so much earlier. But you're here now, that's the main thing,' Jack boomed, a broad smile.

There was a noise coming from my right, a grinding crunching sound of hooves on the loose shingle of the beach. I could see shire horses, pulling a canvassed wagon.

'What are you doing, Jack?' I said, my throat dry.

'They're my horses Johnny, my new pets. I like to do a few things the old-fashioned way. The fuels aren't going to last forever, so I'm going back in time. These beasts can pull pretty much anything you ask them to.'

The wagon drew to a stop, the giant horses' breath pluming in the cold morning air. The villagers circled me, and I saw other faces I recognised. Alison was there, Jack's partner, but no sign of Jefferson, Bob Sack or Griffin. For the most part the villagers just mumbled to themselves and stared at me. Better armed now, battle hardened.

'Jack,' I said. 'Are you itching to kill me?'

'Not me, Johnny,' he answered. 'Them.'

The large canvas sheet covering the wagon fell away. Beneath was a black wrought-iron cage, perhaps ten feet square. Inside were two familiar figures, blackened by remorseless decay, but moving and alert. Looking up into the dead faces of Griffin and his brother Dexter, I felt sick.

'Hold him!' Jack's voice boomed again, as if telepathically reading I was about to bolt.

Rough hands gripped each of my arms, and I looked over at the half-recognised faces either side. They pushed me towards the steps at the rear of the wagon, and a small locked gate in the cage. Jack had a key in his hand. 'I've waited too long for this,' he said. 'Tie his hands!'

'Listen, everybody, before this happens there are things you should know,' I shouted. 'On the rig I met two people, two strangers Alice and Trent. They were behind everything that has happened to you all. They were terrorists ... infected the water in this country with a virus. It turned everyone who was not naturally immune in the walking dead. Are you people listening to me?' I shouted, looking into the blank faces surrounding me. Jack went up to the lock and started to turn the key.

'This man here wants to kill me. Jack Nation, the man who built a fence, a man who with his sadist, twisted son kidnapped and raped my girlfriend. Now he wants to kill the law, and it won't stop there. How many of you will fall out with this man one day, a petty squabble that ends with you tied to a tree or in this fucking cage. Now I don't see a single blood relative of this man alive here today. You all have the power to stop him right now,' I pleaded.

Jack hit me, a hard slap that twisted my head to one side. My face was on fire. 'Lucky I don't cut out your tongue first.'

'Wait,' a female voice said. It was Alison. 'Don't let him go in until I've hurt him too.'

'He's about to get torn to pieces and you want to put the boot in as well. God love you.' Jack's lizard face cracked a smile.

Alison walked out of the crowd and faced me, the woman who had helped me save Toby Hanson at the farm. She had a hunting knife in her hands, the blade glinting silver in the sunrise.

'Where did you get that knife? Now don't cut him too deep, sweetheart; we don't want Griffin and Dexter to go short,' Jack said, edgy.

Looking into Alison's eyes, there was something dead in there, as if they had seen too much. Along the way, she must have lost everything. Killing me would be nothing. She drew the blade up to my neckline. I could feel the blood in my jugular pulsing, terrified. 'It can end now,' she hissed.

'Not the neck,' Jack said, coming forward. Then a look of surprise on his face. All at once, he was on the floor in a pool of red, murmurs from the crowd rising to shouts.

'Throw him in the cage.' Alison's voice cutting through everything. For a second I thought she meant me, but then it was Jack being lifted and carried. He was trying to speak, but instead blood flowed from his mouth, and from around the knife still lodged in his lung. The cage door was slammed behind his prone body, and for a moment, I watched both Dexter and Griffin looking down, hesitant. It was as if some part deep in their rotted synapses remembered their father, the man they would respect and follow to the end of the world. Then, like a breeze, the moment passed, they dropped down like hungry dogs and tore out their breakfast. I watched Jack's wide, helpless eyes until the life dulled out of them. Finally over.

My hands were free, and I looked out over a sea of expectant faces. What do murderers say at times like these, I wondered?

'The terrorists behind the zombies,' I shouted. 'We're going to kill them all.'

They applauded me. It was the new life.

EPILOGUE

The figures crept through the dark and crouched against the rusting chain-link fence. Bolt cutters snipped at the wire, making holes big enough for people and equipment.

'What is this place?' Santiago said to the big man beside him, his comrade.

'It was Greenham Common airbase once upon a time. The Americans stored their Cruise missiles, the women protested and chained themselves to these fences. They closed the place years ago, it's just silos now.'

'Hushhh!' the sound came through their ear pieces. 'Stop talking now.'

They crept forward, slow and steady, clouds in the sky smothering the moon.

'The one in the middle,' the voice came again. 'Santiago, move forward now.'

The young Spaniard ran the last twenty metres and hugged the cool wall of the silo. Walking crab-like he edged up to the door, a heavy metal construct opening by key not padlock. He listened keenly for any sound within. Nothing. Perhaps they had been mistaken this time.

'Open it,' the voice in his ear said.

Santiago took the delicate tools out of the pocket in his black combat jacket. Switching on the dull light of his head torch he sorted through the spindle sticks until his fingers found the one he wanted. He pushed it slowly into the lock and began to knock the lock's levers down one by one. It was a skill that had been hard-earned one hot summer in Madrid, killing the hours during a three month stretch for pickpocketing one stupid tourist too many. Now he was their craftsman.

The lock was defeated. 'Ouvre,' he whispered into the radio mike.

They came in a rush to join him. The wranglers, how he hated their job. It gave him the bad dreams. The men with their long poles and dog collars on the necks of those things. One by one they launched them forward into the black space beyond the open door. half-trained, half-obedient, the wretches disappeared. They could be called back later. Sometimes there were accidents.

Santiago stood with the others and waited. He thought the silo must be empty, that it had been a wasted journey after all. Then the first scream came, followed by more, a cacophony of rising howls and cries for mercy. As always they came running out, some naked, others bitten and sick already, like rats from a ship The lights came on then, blinding halogen to burn their retinas and slow them down.

'Who are you?' one shouted.

The marksmen fired, crisp accurate shots knocking them down like bowling pins. Only children could be spared, but he saw few of those anymore.

Santiago's leader was among the fallen, the pistol in his hand. John never liked it when they played dead. Each one of them got an extra bullet to keep. We had finished with this country now, but the whole world was waiting.

THE END

BIOGRAPHY

Remy Porter is British. He recently emigrated to South Australia with his wife and young daughter. *Dead Beat* is his first novel.

Lightning Source UK Ltd.
Milton Keynes UK
20 August 2010

158755UK00002B/4/P